The Old Beach House
Marilyn Turk

Published by Forget Me Not Romances, an imprint of Winged Publications

ISBN: 9798534286601

"See to it that no one falls short of the grace of God and that no bitter root grows up to cause trouble and defile many." Hebrews 12:15

Chapter One

"C'mon, Courtney. Don't be such a dud." Evan Barnett, Courtney's coworker nudged her shoulder. "Seriously, Drake is watching you."

"You know how I hate these things, Evan." Courtney scanned the room full of conference attendees enjoying cocktail hour. Men in suits and women in business casual clothes clustered in small groups chatting about business. Courtney's insides twisted. She didn't do well with small talk, even about marketing, unless it was in a real meeting.

"Yeah, well, you can pretend to have a good time. By the way, you look great."

"Thanks. I try." She glanced at her reflection in the huge mirror that lined the wall. She had chosen a simple black dress short enough to show off her long legs. Her straight brown hair fell down her back, unrestrained for a change instead of rolled up in her typical work-knot.

"What're you drinking?" Evan eyed her plastic glass.

Courtney looked down at the beverage. "Sparkling water."

Evan rolled his eyes. "A real party girl, aren't

you?"

Courtney grimaced. "That I never claimed to be." Even in college, Courtney had avoided getting involved in the party scene, a trait which didn't help her popularity in the sorority.

Evan lifted his glass. "Cheers!" He frowned. "Uh oh. Guess who is coming this way? Think I'll go find a corner to hide in."

Before she could reply, Mr. Drake, senior vice president of marketing, walked up and peered down at her from the top of his bifocals. "Miss Morgan, you look very nice tonight." He glanced around the room. "You need to go mingle with our clients." He leaned in uncomfortably close to her, lowering his voice. "Especially Mr. Rollins. You should try to get to know him better."

Courtney had no desire to know the old geezer any better. She already knew his biography—sixty-five years old, owner of the largest construction and real estate company in the state, four ex-wives and six children. Couldn't afford to retire with all the alimony and child support he had to pay. His last wife was half his age, but she lasted long enough to get a nice settlement after she caught him cheating on her. Really? Who would want to have a fling with that man? Not Courtney.

Apparently, her face gave away her feelings, because Mr. Drake frowned. "I'm not asking you to sleep with the man, Courtney, that is, unless you want to. But it won't hurt you to be friendly. You know how important his business is to the company."

Courtney's stomach churned. Knowing Mr.

Rollins, he'd assume her "friendliness" was flirting. And to think her boss was so unconcerned about her morality made her ill.

"I mean it, Courtney. Get over yourself and go talk to him." Mr. Drake fixed her with a glare. "You *do* want to make it to senior marketing manager, don't you?" He turned and strode away.

Her blood boiled at her boss's threat, and her face grew hot. She'd worked hard for this company for the past six years, ever since getting her graduate degree in marketing, climbing the ranks to her current position. To think her future depended on whether she was friendly with a client, especially an obnoxious old man, infuriated her. She wouldn't do it. She wouldn't kowtow to Mr. Drake's threats. What would he do to her if she didn't obey his command? Fire her? Surely not.

Chapter Two

Courtney tripped over the broken walkway before climbing the steps to the old beach house, tugging her suitcase behind her. Tucker, her golden retriever, trotted at her side. The wooden porch creaked under their feet as she fumbled with the keys. She jiggled the knob before it eventually gave way and opened.

"Achoo!" She waved away the dust motes that danced in the sunlight. Business cards that had been stuck in the door fell at her feet, so she scooped them up, noticing the names of realtors as she shoved them in her jean pocket. "This place needs a good cleaning," she said, as if Tucker understood. He wagged his tail in response.

She pulled the blinds up on the windows to let more light in the front of the house before entering the large family room. Tucker raced ahead into the room and began sniffing everything in sight. Courtney jerked dust-laden sheets off the furniture as memories flooded her mind. Gazing at the odd assortment—chairs with faded upholstery, a rattan loveseat, bamboo rockers, and an overstuffed recliner —she envisioned the people who used to

4

occupy them. She smiled at the lamp with the red-and-white lighthouse base, a testimony to her grandmother's love of lighthouses. A long farmer's table ran along one side of the room. How many times had she and her brother Clay sat there with Mom and Dad, Grandma and Grandpa, and an assortment of aunts, uncles, and cousins as they worked on puzzles or played games together?

Her eyes misted, wetting her eyelashes. Where had the time gone? Where had everybody gone? In the ten years since they'd all been together, Grandma and Grandpa had both passed away, Clay had gotten married and lived on the other side of the country, her parents traveled all the time, and her cousins had grown and scattered to the far corners of the world. Meanwhile, Courtney had finished her bachelor's and master's degrees before enjoying a successful career in marketing. Her stomach tightened. Well, for six years it was successful. But now even that was questionable, much less enjoyable.

No one cared about the rambling old beach cottage anymore, the place her grandparents had loved to share with their family. Once a place of joy, it had been relegated to the past like some childhood toy. How lonely the house must be, if houses could be lonely. Or maybe she was just transferring her own feelings to the house. Alone and cast aside. Wasn't that what she was?

Mr. Drake had made good on his threat when she didn't play the schmoozing game with Mr. Rollins. Of course, the official reason for her departure a week after the party was a "reduction in force," and her position was being eliminated. She had no doubt the real reason was retaliation for her insubordination, especially since he'd had no communication with her since the party. Shocked by his vindictiveness, she'd been crushed to find out how little she meant to the company.

She'd cried for days, praying and asking God how He had allowed this to happen to her. After all, she had done nothing wrong. She had been a good girl, a good employee, and avoided any situation that might have been compromising. Why was she being punished for that? Why did God allow her plans to be destroyed?

Anger competed with depression in her heart and mind. She seethed with thoughts of getting back at Mr. Drake, as well as ways to get even. She even asked God to punish the man. He shouldn't be allowed to get away with what he did to her. But who cared what he did? Who cared if she was let go? Only Evan and a couple of other co-workers in her department. But they'd never speak out about Drake's actions.

When Courtney told her parents about being let go, they begged her to come home. But she knew she'd be assaulted by questions about what happened and what she planned to do about her future. While praying about what to do, a picture of the beach house came to her mind. When she asked her parents if she could go there, they reluctantly agreed, but were concerned about the condition, apologizing for not having taken better care of as it. A local realtor had agreed to check on the house occasionally for them, hoping someday they'd allow him to sell it.

Courtney didn't care what the cottage looked like now. It was the one place only happy things had happened, and she needed something happy, something to take her mind off the whole job situation. She had to get away from the city, the Mr. Drakes of the world, and everything that had defined her for the last few years. When she decided to come to the beach house, a weight had lifted from her. She didn't know what she'd do next, but at the beach house, she wouldn't worry about it. Thanks to her former level with the company, she had a nice exit package plus her savings to last her a while.

Courtney rolled her big suitcase into the middle of the room and carried her large tote bag to the kitchen that opened off the family room. She chuckled at Grandpa's foresight to make the house so open, long before the open floor plan was popular. The old house was deceivingly large inside compared to its modest cottage appearance on the front, and had seven bedrooms total, four upstairs and three down. From her tote bag, she retrieved Tucker's bowl, her coffee maker and favorite mug. She placed the machine on the counter and her dog's dish on the floor. Then she filled them both with bottled water she'd brought. She plugged in the coffee maker and pushed the start button. Thank goodness, the real estate office had turned on the electricity before she arrived. After the long drive here, she craved a cup of fresh coffee. But first, she needed to clean off the counter, no doubt laden with dust.

Finding a dish towel in a drawer, she turned on the kitchen faucet. After some coughing and gurgling, water finally spurted out. She rummaged under the sink for some dish soap and set to wiping off the counter while Tucker lapped up his water. When the coffee maker was ready, she added a K-cup, put her mug in place, and pushed the button. The aroma of hot coffee soon filled the room, like a homecoming party encouraging her to sit, relax and savor the brew.

Cleaning the rest of the place could wait until later. Right now, she was anxious to go out on the back porch and see the water. She grabbed her mug, opened the door to the screened in porch and stepped out, greeted by the sea breeze that forced its way in. The view of the water was enough to lift her spirits, despite all that had happened to get her there.

Inhaling the fresh air, she stood with hands cupped around her mug, allowing the sound of the waves splashing onto the shore to establish the rhythm of her heart. She glanced around the large porch and recognized furniture that had always been there—an old glider on one end and a picnic table on the other. In between were four Adirondack chairs. She propped the door to the house open so the fresh air would reach the interior and remove some of the mustiness. Then, taking a seat at the picnic table, she took a long sip of coffee and gazed out at the turquoise water of the Gulf of Mexico. Tucker came to sit beside her and nudged her hand. She recognized the signal and patted his head.

"Well, boy, what are we going to do now?"

He wagged his tail, obviously content to do whatever she suggested.

She checked her phone and saw a message. Must be mom. She picked it up and listened. "Courtney? Did you make it safely to the cottage? How does it look? Do you need anything? Just let me know. Daddy and I are worried about you. Call me to let me know you're all right. Love you!"

Courtney texted back, "I'm here and I'm okay. TTYL. Love, C." She set down the phone. She'd call Mom later when she felt like talking. The afternoon sun was beginning its descent, and couples walked hand-in-hand down the beach. A twinge of self-pity pricked her heart. Why wasn't she part of a couple? Was something wrong with her? But then her sensible side talked back to her emotions. She had made the choices necessary for her education and career and hadn't wanted anything to derail her plans. In college, a few nice guys in college had asked her out, but she never allowed anything to get beyond a platonic relationship.

A lot of good it did her now. Single, alone and unemployed. Wow. This was never in her plans. The old "master of my fate, captain of my soul" phrase had been so popular when she was in college. She really had thought she was the master of her own fate. Captain of her soul? Not so much. That was one title she had given to God years ago.

She finished her coffee while the beach beckoned.

"I need to stretch my legs, Tucker. Would you like to go for a walk?"

The retriever wagged his whole body at the mention of one of his favorite activities. Courtney found his leash and attached it to his collar. She kicked off her shoes, opened the screen door, and they carefully navigated the warped back steps. The Morgan beach house was one of the few that still had some semblance of a yard, marked off by a weathered picket fence that surrounded the house and did a fair job of keeping more sand from encroaching the yard that was mostly beach grass and sea oats, except for some wild roses close to the porch.

Opening the fence gate, she stepped onto the soft sand, allowing it to sift between her toes like sugar. At once she was a child again, breathing the salt air and absorbing the sight and sound of the surf. Tucker bounded toward the water, and she trotted behind to keep up with him. Spotting some sandpipers at the edge of the surf, he sprang after them. "Woof! Woof!"

"They can run faster than you, Tucker!" Courtney laughed as the birds' tiny legs raced down the shore away from the dog before taking flight.

A seagull squawked overhead as if taunting the dog, and Tucker followed its flight, barking at it too.

"Come on, boy, let's get some exercise."

Courtney started jogging on the wet sand with Tucker at her side, darting around other people walking on the beach. As she ran, knots of tension that had built up in her dissipated and blew away with the sea breeze that played with her hair. And to think she used to pay a masseuse to rid her of that tightness in her neck and back. She smiled, enjoying the freedom of being unshackled from the corporate world. Why would she ever want to return?

The sun was a golden orb slipping into the water when Courtney stopped jogging. Tucker sat down beside her as she paused to watch the sun melt into the horizon, streaking the sky and tinting the clouds in streaks of oranges, reds, golds and pinks. Sunsets over the water had always captivated her, and she'd missed seeing their awesome splendor. What a shame so many people missed that glorious sight. Years ago, when the whole family sat in beach chairs behind the cottage to observe it, Grandpa would say, "Nobody can watch a sunset and not believe in God." If only that were true. Incredibly, she had met those who didn't believe and credited science with the amazing phenomenon.

She turned around and they headed back toward the cottage. With no one on the beach but the two of them, Courtney unhooked Tucker's leash, so he had more freedom to run. The dog was well-trained, and she knew he would stay near her. He stopped to lap some of the seawater along the way, but saltwater wouldn't quench his thirst.

"Sorry, buddy. Next time, I'll bring a bottle of water on our walks. Because we *will* be doing this again. And often."

Jogging back, her attention was drawn to the other houses on the beach. A mixture of emotions flooded her at the changes that had occurred in the ten years since she'd last been there. The 1940's beach houses that previously dotted the shore had been replaced with gleaming glass and stone structures, cold and uninviting, in her opinion. Where empty lots had been, new homes stood, leaving little space between each one. As she reached her family's house, the difference between it and its neighbors stood out. The old-school white clapboard cottage with a screened-in back porch appeared antiquated and misplaced. It was as if everything from the past had disappeared except for that one house and returning to it was like stepping back into another era.

But she loved the old place, the feel of the past. And if it were up to her, it would never change.

Chapter Three

Jared Freeman threw his backpack onto the sofa and walked toward the sliding glass doors of his condo. Stepping outside on the balcony, he sucked in the fresh salt air and scanned the darkening horizon. His weekend in Air Force reservist duty was complete until next month when he reported again.

He looked forward to these weekends when he could get back into the air and reconnect with flying. Throughout college at the Air Force Academy, he'd dreamed of being an Air Force pilot and thought that would be his career. If life had gone according to his plans, that would have been the case. However, after eight years in, Dad was diagnosed with cancer, so Jared had requested a "humanitarian reassignment" to move his duty station from California to Florida to be near his parents. But the Air Force refused his request, and Jared had no choice but to leave. As the only child, he was the only one his parents could rely on.

Ironically, thanks to the Air Force's "palace chase" program, he was able to transition to a reserve unit in Florida and still keep his rank as

Captain. So here he was, back home in Serendipity working in his father's real estate business. It wasn't a bad job, especially being so near the beach every day. But the important thing was being there for Dad and Mom too. She wore out the highway taking Dad to Houston for treatments once a month to hold the cancer at bay. Dad tried to stay upbeat, mainly for her sake, but dealing with the illness had taken its toll on both of them. Jared offered to take him instead, but Mom wanted to spend every minute with him that she could. Jared was in awe of his parents' love and devotion for each other. Was that kind of love even possible anymore?

Two of the four marriages he'd been a groomsman in had already fallen apart. After less than five years! Maybe it was his fault, and it was just bad luck to have him in a wedding. After all, he was the lone ranger. Every time he met someone he was kind of interested in, the initial attraction wore off. The longest he'd dated anyone was a year, and then off and on because of his active-duty assignments. And since he'd been back in Florida, he never met any single women because his clients were married and buying houses for their families.

Sure, there were singles' hangouts around the Serendipity beach, but he'd never enjoyed the fake friendliness of bars, the women who had had too much plastic surgery to look normal, and the way they attached themselves to the old rich guys. Besides, he detested watching people get drunk. Didn't they know what idiots they looked like? Apparently not. But he guessed if everyone else was getting drunk and acting stupid, they didn't notice when others did. No, the wedding receptions he'd attended were enough party for him. And no expectations.

Jared went back inside, unzipped his olive drab flight suit, walked to the bedroom and let it drop to the floor. He grabbed a pair of shorts and a T-shirt for a late afternoon run. It'd be dark in about twenty minutes, so he better hurry. Throwing on his tennis shoes, he hurried out the door and trotted down two flights of steps to the bottom floor. He headed to the shoreline and took off down the beach, savoring the sound of the gentle surf as it brushed the sand. Here on the Gulf Coast, the waves seldom got large or angry like they did on the other coasts, and when they did, it meant a storm was nearby. Normally, the waves weren't much good for surfing, unless you were crazy enough to get out in a tropical storm like the desperate surfers did.

He ran ten minutes in one direction, then turned around and retraced his steps back home. Lights were appearing along the beach in the windows of the houses with full time residents. The houses that were available for rent would be full in another month. For now, he'd enjoy the relative quiet. Most of the houses were new construction or renovations of older ones. The sleepy seaside town of his youth had morphed into a vacation mecca for the wealthy.

As he neared the old Morgan cottage, he was surprised to see a couple of lights in it too. Who could that be? The place had been shut up for years, ever since its original owners, James and Helen Morgan had passed away. In fact, most of the original residents in the area had died, and their property had been sold to newcomers. Jared was one of the few bona fide locals, having been born and raised there, an oddity among the multitudes who had moved to the beach from somewhere else.

A dog barked, sounding as if it came from the screen porch as he passed by the house. So who was there? He'd had such great times there when he was a kid. He'd played with Clay and Courtney Morgan and their cousins who came for the summer. They'd spent hours on the beach, playing in the sand, trying to surf or skim board, and having cookouts over bonfires. At night, they'd laid out and studied the stars, identifying constellations and planets in the dark sky unspoiled by streetlights. Back then, there weren't any streetlights and there were far less houses. The kids had pretended to be on a desert island, and nobody knew where they were. That is, until someone's parents called them to come in.

He smiled at the memory. Whatever happened to Clay and Courtney? They were probably married with children like everyone else his age by now. He'd always thought Courtney was kind of cute, but they'd teased her and told her she looked like a blue heron with her long lanky legs. She'd been taller than the rest of them back then, especially him, since he didn't start growing vertically until high school. Her nickname was Stringbean, "Bean" for short, and she'd taken the teasing well, calling him Shrimp, because he was so small. He winced at the name. No one would call him that now.

Jared studied the old house, the only one of its kind still on the beach. Years ago, many of the houses look the same. But now, the old style was a relic standing out among its new, modern neighbors. The family should sell the place and let someone put a really nice new house there. Since the property was prime real estate, the family would get a pretty penny for its sale. Why wouldn't they sell it if no one used it? Maybe there were new owners in there now. As far as he knew, the Morgan house was not a rental, but if there had been a sale, surely he would have heard about it.

Capturing that sale would be quite a feather in his cap. Not only would he make an awesome commission, Dad would be proud of his success in the business. Jared could be a good salesman if he wanted to be, but he hadn't really tried. He had mainly just kept things going at the office, deferring the competition to the agents that worked for them. The real estate market in the area was fierce, and agents watched the movement of property like a hawk, ready to pounce on its prey. Deaths and divorces provided opportunities for some, hardship for others, a reality Jared ruefully admitted. Space on the beach was limited, and every square inch was desirable, even to the extent that larger lots had been divided to get more houses on them. He was amazed at what people would pay to have beachfront property.

All this beach-grabbing frenzy had created a new problem—property rights. Those who had paid the premium for their own footprint in the sand, wanted to claim every grain of sand as their own. Much to the chagrin of beachgoers who just wanted to enjoy a day near the water, these property owners had set up signs and boundary ropes claiming private property to keep those pesky tourists off their precious land. As a result, the county had set up public parking areas on the street with pockets of beach access. However, the public beach was often not as wide as the private beach next to it, so the occasional beach chair often trespassed, provoking the owners.

Jared hated all this conflict. The beach was supposed to be a place people came for relaxation. In the past, those with beachfront homes never complained about sharing their property with others. The water didn't belong to anyone but God, and the shoreline moved with the tide. How someone could claim that area was beyond him. Still, there was an ongoing battle and pressure on the county to restrict tourist encroachment. How sad. Why couldn't things be the way they used to be when everyone enjoyed the beach together?

His own condo was an exception to the area of high-priced homes. Grandfathered into the zoning, the three-story condo building had once been one of Serendipity's first beach motels, a rare bargain for the average beachgoer. But five years ago, the owners had converted it into condos, renovating the units and selling them. There were only fifteen units in the complex, and they were snatched up pretty quickly. Most of the buyers quickly turned them into rental units, capitalizing on their investment. Lucky for him, his father had been one of them, so Jared now lived on the beach, rent-free even, since Dad wouldn't accept any rent from him. But Jared wouldn't accept any payment for working with the real estate office, so they called it even.

As he climbed the stairs to his place, he thought about the Morgan cottage again. He was eager to see what he could find out at the office tomorrow.

Chapter Four

Courtney spent the next day cleaning. She'd twisted her hair up in a knot and wore an old University of Florida Gator T-shirt and black yoga pants. Her phone set on high volume to hear her play list, she sang along with Lauren Daigle as she vacuumed.

"You say I am loved," she sang loudly, as she embraced the words of the song. Over the din, she thought she heard Tucker barking. She turned off the vacuum and glanced around to find the dog.

"Tucker! What's up?" He stood by the front door and looked back at her as if she should come see the object of his concern.

She lowered the volume. Who knew she was here? It must be the real estate office that took care of the property for them coming to see if everything was all right. She peeked through the window without getting too close to be seen as she checked out her visitor. She couldn't see his face, but the body was nice. A navy polo shirt and khaki shorts revealed the muscular, trim guy with sandy brown hair. He was pretty tall, at least taller than she was, which was always nice. What was she thinking?

Since when did she care about a random stranger at her door? Still, she wished she'd put on a drop of makeup this morning.

"Tucker, stay," she said, pointing to the dog as she grabbed the doorknob.

Pulling it open halfway, she stared into a gorgeous pair of light blue eyes.

The guy smiled. "Hello, I'm from Coastal Real Estate. We've been handling the property here for the Morgans. Not that we've done much, but we've kept an eye on the place to make sure no one bothered it. We got a call to turn on the electricity, so I wanted to make sure everything worked."

The voice was familiar, and the face slightly so. She looked at the shirt and saw Jared Freeman on a name tag opposite the Coastal Real Estate logo. Her eyes widened.

"Shrimp?" got out of her mouth before she could stop herself.

His eyes registered shock, and he looked her up and down. "Bean?"

Courtney's hands covered her mouth. "Oh my gosh! You can't be Jared Freeman!"

He grinned and nodded. "'Fraid so. But man, Bean, have you changed!"

Now she was really embarrassed. She glanced down at her clothes and shrugged. "Sorry, I'm a mess. The place needed cleaning. Apparently, your company didn't handle that."

His face reddened. "No, I'm afraid that's not part of the contract. We've just kept the grass mowed in the little yard out front and checked on it periodically. Actually, we don't usually watch property for people. But my father really admired your grandfather and told him he'd make sure the place was okay. He passed away, didn't he?" At her nod, he continued. "I'm sorry. He was such a nice man. So I guess we've been dealing with your father?"

"Yes, that's right. Unfortunately, Mom and Dad haven't come to Serendipity in years. I feel bad about the old place being empty so long." She suddenly realized she wasn't being hospitable by not inviting him in. "Would you like to come in? I don't have much here, but I can make you a cup of coffee."

He hesitated and glanced at his watch. "Sure. I'd like to hear what you've been up to."

She cringed inwardly. Must she tell him the whole sorry story about being let go? But, this was Shrimp, that is, Jared, an old friend. He sure wasn't a shrimp anymore. Quite the contrary in fact. And frankly, right now, an old friend sounded like the best kind of friend to be around. She stepped back from the door to let him in.

"Hey, guy." Jared leaned over to pet Tucker. Tucker wagged his tail, an instant friend.

"That's Tucker."

"Beautiful dog. I've always liked golden retrievers, just never had one. Mother had a thing about too much animal hair in the house."

Courtney smiled. "I understand. He does shed a lot. But it comes with the territory. And he's a great companion." Did she sound too needy?

"I bet. I wouldn't mind having a pet, but my schedule has been a bit irregular, plus my place isn't that large."

Courtney walked to the coffee pot and turned it on. She found a mug in the cabinet, took it down, rinsed it out, then set it under the coffee spout. "I hope you like strong coffee."

"Why drink anything else?" He walked over to stand beside her as the coffee dripped.

Her pulse quickened by his closeness, and she stepped to the fridge to get the creamer, not to mention, catch her breath. Since when did Jared Freeman have this effect on her?

"Creamer?" She set it on the counter.

"No thanks. I drink it black." He took the cup of coffee she handed him.

"I can't do it black. I have to add a little something." She popped a new K-cup in the pot and set her own mug under the brewer. While it brewed, Jared glanced around.

"Man, this really brings back memories. How long has it been since anyone was here?"

She fixed her coffee, then picked up her cup. "Ten years. Can you believe it?"

"Feels like a lifetime ago," he said.

"I know. It's so strange coming back here as an adult, remembering it as a child."

She walked toward the back porch, and he followed her. As he stepped out, he blew out a breath. "Man. Déjà vu."

Courtney switched on the ceiling fan and sat down at the picnic table. Jared joined her at the other end facing the beach. "I can't believe so much has changed around here. It feels like the house got sucked out of an era and plopped down into a new one."

"You're right. None of the old gang is around anymore."

"Nor any of the houses they stayed in." Courtney sipped her coffee.

"Not on the beach at least. The oldest houses are on Main Street."

"Yeah. Serendipity is one of the most popular beach communities to live in now, thanks to a poll that circled the Internet."

"In that case, I guess you stay busy selling property."

He gave her a wry smile. "I could be if I wanted to be more aggressive. There's enough agents around here doing that already."

Courtney remembered the cards she'd picked up when she arrived. She'd sifted through them and found they were all from real estate agents. "I believe it. There was a bunch of cards left on the front door."

"I'm not surprised. This is a prime piece of real estate. Do you think your folks would ever sell?"

Courtney cut him a glance. Was that why he was here? "Not if I have anything to do with it." Did her response sound as sharp as it felt?

"Hey, I don't blame you. I'd hate to see this place go. And you know it would. I seriously doubt a new buyer would keep it as it is. It'd either be renovated or torn down and rebuilt."

Courtney grimaced. Her stomach clenched with the thought of someone doing that.

"I'm not sure why Dad has kept it all these years. I guess he's still attached too, even though they haven't been here for so long."

"So how are your parents? What have they been doing?" Jared's happy manner was a welcome change.

"Traveling. When Clay and I moved away, Dad retired, and they travel all the time. When they're not going across the country in their RV, they're cruising somewhere."

"Nice." He glanced down at his coffee.

Courtney sensed a shift in his mood. "And your parents?"

His face was somber. "Dad's got cancer. That's really why I moved back here, to help him out at the business."

"Oh, I'm so sorry to hear that." What should she say?

"He's in remission right now, but he doesn't have the energy he used to have, and Mom won't leave his side. They have to go to Texas every month to check his status, and that's a drain on both of them."

"That's tough. I'm sure he's thankful you're here though."

"He is. But I'm the only child. What choice did I have?"

Courtney's heart went out to him.

"What were you doing before?"

Jared explained to her about being in the Air Force and having to resign to get close to home. "But I still get to fly, so it worked out."

"That's good." She didn't think he was really happy about the way things had worked out though. "So, are you married?" She didn't see a ring on his finger but had come to realize that not all married men wore rings, for one reason or another. She probably wouldn't have asked any other guy that question, but after all, this was just Jared, and they were just friends.

"No. You know what they say, 'Always a groomsman, but never a groom'?"

Courtney laughed. "I never heard it said exactly that way, but I get it."

"Seriously, I just never seemed to have time for a serious relationship with school and deployments. You?"

She shook her head. "I'm sort of the same. College, master's degree, then climbing the corporate ladder."

His eyebrows lifted. "I never could see myself in that world. Our little company here is big enough for me. So, are you here taking a break from the corporate action?"

"You might say so." She didn't feel like telling him anymore about that story now. "But guess who's a family man? Clay! Can you believe it? He has two children now and lives in Colorado."

Jared laughed. "Clay, wow. Can't picture it. He must've grown some responsibility."

"Yes, he did. Got a degree in engineering and married a really nice girl he met in college. Her family lives in North Carolina. I have pictures on my phone. Let me go get it." She stood and lifted her cup. "More coffee?"

He stood as well. "No, thank you." He pulled his phone from his back pocket and glanced at it. "This thing's been buzzing constantly. I better find out what the *emergency* is. I didn't mean to stay so long, but the time got away from me."

"Sure. Let me take that." She reached for his cup.

They went back inside, and she put the cups in the sink. Picking up her phone, she scrolled to the pictures of Clay with his family and showed them to Jared.

"Nice family. Good for him."

"Yes, I'm happy for my little brother."

"He's not so little anymore."

"Ha! Finally outgrew me." She glanced at him as she walked him to the door.

"So did I," Jared said. "Finally."

Boy, had he. Who would've thought?

She opened the door for him, and he stepped out, then turned around. "You know, Courtney—I can't call you Bean anymore—I've really enjoyed seeing you again. Catching up."

"I enjoyed talking with you too. Thanks for giving me a break from my cleaning."

"Would you like to get together again some time? There's a great restaurant near here, and if we hit it during the week, we'll avoid the crazy crowds."

"That sounds great. I haven't seen much around here except the beach."

"How soon are you going back to the corporate world?"

"I don't know yet." And that was the truth.

Chapter Five

Jared couldn't shake the image of Courtney out of his mind. How had she gotten so, so gorgeous? Even with her hair messed up and no make-up, she was just naturally pretty. He never dreamed she'd grow up to be so stunning. If he'd known, maybe he wouldn't have given her such a hard time when they were kids. Sure. He was just being a kid like she was. Thank God they'd both grown out of their nicknames. She was still tall, but she was no string bean anymore, having filled out in all the right places.

He shook his head. Wow. It almost felt like old times being together again in the old beach house. Almost, except they were the only two there, and now they were adults. Even though they hadn't seen each other in years, they still shared that childhood bond of friendship. Both had grown and changed and in many ways they were strangers, but the magnetic pull of camaraderie drew them together. But if it hadn't been their shared past, he still would've been attracted to her. No other woman had caught his eye like she did.

But what of her love life? She said she had been

too busy like he had been, but maybe there was someone now. She'd acted rather enigmatic, if not a tad irritated, when he asked her about taking a break from the corporate scene. He assumed she needed a vacation, but what if it she was getting over a boyfriend? One she might be going back to. Had Jared acted too eager to see her again? He wasn't normally like that. Shoot, what an idiot. On the other hand, she said she wanted to get together again too. Of course, for old times' sake, nothing more.

When he arrived at the family's office built in a craftsman-style design, Marla, the receptionist frowned. "Making house calls again, Jared?"

No doubt she was alluding to one of their clients, Merrilee Chambers, a long-time client of the firm that demanded extra attention. Since his father had gotten ill, she had called to see him often on the ruse of buying more property or getting advice about real estate dealings. The fifty-something widow was loaded, thanks to her late husband who was twenty-five years her senior and had left her with more money than she knew what to do with. Even before his death, she'd been nipped, tucked, and shaped all over, producing the fake body of a thirty-year-old. Jared's father had coddled her to keep her from taking her money elsewhere. However, now her sights were set on Jared, and he bristled at her flirtations. He believed the term that applied to her was "cougar."

"Yes, as a matter of fact. I was at the Morgan house," thankful to say he wasn't at Merrilee's. "One of the Morgan family members was there, an old friend, so we took a few minutes to catch up." Best not mention the Morgan was female and give the women in the office something to gossip about. "Why?"

"I transferred some calls to your desk phone and left a couple on your cell. Haven't you checked it?"

"I got so many messages, I haven't had time to get through them yet." The office was only a mile from the Morgan house after all.

"I'll save you the trouble. You know the Richardsons that live next door to the Morgan's house? Well, they complained of a dog barking. Said it barked all night and they were planning to call the police if it happened again. The dog was apparently at the Morgan house."

"Geez." Jared thought of Tucker, who'd barked at him before the door was opened. But he hadn't barked once afterwards.

He headed toward his desk, but Marla spoke behind him. "There's more." He paused and turned around. "The Cunninghams saw a young woman running on the beach with a dog and didn't see a collar. They questioned if the dog had a permit to be on the beach. I wonder if it was the same dog."

Good grief. They must be talking about Tucker too, since he was a "new" dog on the beach. Courtney probably didn't even know about the permit. He'd have to let her know. Shock stopped him in his tracks. He didn't have her number. He really was an idiot. Who asks a girl out then fails to get her number? Yours truly. Oh well, the upside to his blunder meant he'd have to see her again, so maybe that wasn't such a bad thing.

"Oh, and Merrilee called." Marla rolled her eyes. "She said it's urgent."

Jared frowned. "Urgent?"

"Umhum."

"All right. I'll call her."

Jared sat down at his desk and read over all his messages before calling Merrilee. He breathed a silent prayer before punching in the number. *Lord, please give me patience and wisdom to handle her problem.*

She must have been holding the phone because she answered as soon as the ring began.

"Jared! Is that you, darlin'?" Her over-the-top southern accent curled his toes. "I've been waitin' all day to hear from you!"

"Sorry, Merrilee. I was tied up with other business." Why did she think she was their only client? Maybe because she wanted to be. "What's the problem?"

"Jared, I think my pool has a leak in it." Her voice sounded tragic.

"Have you called the pool service?" No, that would be too logical.

"Well, no. I wanted you to come look at it for me and see if you can tell what the problem is."

"I'm not a pool expert, Merrilee. You really should call the pool company.

"But Jared, if your daddy was feeling better, I know he'd come look at it for me." Of course, she played the old "dad" card. How did his dad, much less his mom, put up with this woman?

"All right, Merrilee. I'll come by later. I need to catch up on some things here at the office first."

"You're a dear. I'll be waiting with bells on!"

She probably wasn't too far from the truth. After all, she did wear some strange clothes sometime and had a thing for leopard. He shook his head and lowered his phone. But before he could set it on the desk, it rang again, and "Mom" was displayed.

"Hi Mom. What's up?"

"Nothing really, honey. Dad just wanted me to call and see if you took care of Merrilee's problem yet."

"Are you serious? She called Dad?" His blood boiled at the woman's insensitivity.

"Oh, Jared. Don't get so upset. She couldn't get you to return her call, so she called your father. He doesn't mind. Is everything okay there?"

"Yes, Mom. Everything is fine. I went to the Morgan house this morning and Courtney Morgan was there, so we talked a while."

"Courtney? Here? By herself? What is she doing these days?"

"She's good." What an understatement. "I just can't believe how much she's changed."

"Is that good? You know you've both grown up since you last saw each other."

"That's the truth." And yes, that was good. Very good. "I think she's here to take a vacation from her corporate job. I'll tell you more about it when I see you."

"You're coming by for dinner tonight, aren't you?" Mom had a way of making him feel like a little boy again, the way she wanted to take care of him.

"Sure, Mom. After I go to Merrilee's. I hope that won't take long. You know, she could have called someone else, like a pool company." He tapped his pen on a notepad.

"I know, dear. She could always call someone else. I think she's just lonely, and this is how she gets attention. Try not to judge her too harshly."

Jared's mother was a saint. She always thought the best of everyone. That gene must've missed him.

Marla went out for lunch and brought him back a sandwich while he returned phone calls. It was four o'clock before he could leave.

"Wish me luck," he said to Marla as he left the office.

Merrilee's house was two miles down the beach in a gated neighborhood. When Jared's car approached the stone columns of the gate, the attendant waved him through. He drove to the last house in the neighborhood, one of the few that was actually on the beach. The place was massive, Merrilee's Taj Mahal that her late husband had built for her. The mansion boasted three floors with two pools— rooftop infinity pool and another pool downstairs outside the living room.

Strangely, there were only four bedrooms, but they were huge and each one had its own spa-like bathroom and a view of the water because the back of the house was all glass. The house had a four-car garage and a separate carriage house, in case they needed extra bedrooms for guests. Jared wondered how many times it had been used, since Mr. Chambers only had two grown sons from a previous marriage, and Jared heard they didn't get along well with their stepmother.

He pulled into the circular drive and parked in front, then trotted up the steps to the oversized double front door. An automatic sensor recognized his presence and rang the doorbell. Before the door opened, the yippy bark of Merrilee's Pomeranian announced his presence. Within minutes, a sun-darkened, platinum-haired Merrilee appeared, wine glass in hand, white yippy dog in the other, wearing a tight-fitting leopard print one-piece thing. Was that called a jumpsuit? She grinned at him revealing perfect laser-white teeth behind her plumped up red lips. Batting her long fake eyelashes, she grabbed his arm and pulled him inside.

"Jared, I'm so glad you're here." Yippee dog growled. "Hush, Sweet Pea! You know Jared! Just pet him, Jared, and he'll know you're a friend."

Jared lifted his hand toward the dog, but Sweet Pea bared her teeth, so he dropped his hand. "Hi Merrilee. Sorry you had to wait."

"Some things are worth waiting for," she teased in her thick southern accent.

Trying to keep his lunch down, he swallowed hard. "So, show me where the problem is."

"Oh, you're just all business, now, aren't you? No time for a little visit? How about a glass of wine? It's the very best vintage, you know."

He had nothing against wine, but he was not making a social call. "Sorry, Merrilee, I don't drink on the job."

"Well, then, honey, just clock yourself out and relax!"

Gag. He faked a laugh. "Sorry, I can't do that now. I have some paperwork to do later, and I need to be clearheaded." *Sorry, God, that was a little fib, but he was short on excuses.*

"Oh, all right. Party pooper!" She gulped some wine, then grinned.

"I forgot to ask which pool you're having trouble with – the upstairs pool or the one downstairs."

"You know, I think you better check both of them."

Trying to keep from showing his annoyance, he shrugged. "Okay. Lead the way."

Feeling like Joseph dealing with Potiphar's wife, he followed her to the glass elevator to the side of the living room where she pushed the button to the top floor. When he stepped out of the elevator, bright sunshine greeted him and an unhindered view of the Gulf of Mexico. He walked to the pool, noticing a towel lying on one of the luxury chaise lounge chairs. Next to the chaise was a small table with a book. Merrilee must lay out in the sun every day. He was curious about her choice in books, but not curious enough to ask. He had to keep this call as professional as possible.

He knew a little about pools from his teenage days as a lifeguard, but very little. Pools were a lot more high-tech now, so what he knew about pumps, etc. was outdated. Still, he dropped his keys on the table and pretended to check things out, walked around, knelt down, felt the water, anything he could think of to assuage Merrilee. She followed him around, chattering mindlessly about trivia.

Mom was probably right. Why would anyone want to live in such an enormous house by themselves? She probably was lonely. He preferred to not be the one that appeased that loneliness, but he could at least be polite.

"Well, Merrilee, I can't find a problem up here. Let's take a look at the downstairs pool."

"Sure, honey. Take your time."

He gritted his teeth. He could be spending his time doing something productive, like calling a pool guy.

They went back downstairs to the lap pool that the living room glass doors opened onto. A stone feature with a waterfall trickled at one end, surrounded by tropical plants. He repeated the scene, checking everything including the waterfall.

He stood up and brushed off his hands. "Nope. Can't find anything. Tell you what. I'll call Wyatt's Pool Care for you. They'll be right over tomorrow and check it out. They know what they're doing."

Merrilee pouted. "You mean you have to leave already?"

He checked his phone. "Yes, Mom and Dad are expecting me for dinner. And I don't want them to have to wait on me." He strode to the door, wishing he could run past through the vast living room with the long white sectional and the stone fireplace that covered one wall. Sticking his hand in his pocket, he froze. No keys. Rats!

"I left my keys upstairs." He headed to the elevator.

Merrilee laughed as she followed him. "Looks like you're supposed to stay longer."

They got on the elevator and rode to the top. He hurried to the table and bent over to pick up the keys. When he stood up, his gaze moved to the beach. His breath caught at the sight. Courtney was running along the shore, Tucker by her side. She was grace in motion with her long, now lovely legs, her long brown hair flying behind her.

"What cha lookin' at, honey?" Merrilee came up beside him. "Who's that? I saw her yesterday."

"I think it's someone I know," he said, not wanting to discuss Courtney with Merrilee.

"Well, wave!"

At that moment, Courtney glanced up. He raised his hand just as Merrilee put her arm around him and waved with the other like she was waving to a Mardi Gras float. "Hi!"

As Courtney looked away, Merrilee said, "I hope that dog doesn't do his business in my yard. We don't allow that around here, do we, Jared?"

Chapter Six

It felt so good to run again. Back in middle school and high school, she had run track, but it had been a long time since then. After a long day of cleaning the cottage, Courtney couldn't wait to get outside and stretch her legs in the fresh air. Tucker needed exercise too, and this was good for both of them. She ran farther than the night before, taking advantage of the deserted beach.

Her thoughts kept going back to Jared. What a surprise he'd been. She'd really enjoyed talking with him, feeling so comfortable around him. She hadn't had that feeling with anyone else for a long time. Seemed like everyone always wanted something from her, and she had to perform her role just right. But with Jared, she could be herself and not worry. She looked forward to seeing him again and getting to know each other better as adults. He was a nice guy, always had been, but his devotion to his parents was admirable. How many young guys would give up their careers to come home and help their parents?

And he was unattached. Not that she was interested in a relationship with him, but she would like to spend time with him and catch up. No strings. If memory served her, his parents used to be active in the local church. Were they still? Maybe not, with his father's illness. What about Jared? Did he attend church too? From her experience, it was rare to see a young single man in church by himself. Maybe while she was staying here, she'd check out the church. She'd passed it on the way to town and thought it quaint, just as it'd always been, small and white with a steeple—the way churches used to look. She'd had enough of mega churches and vast congregations. A small community church appealed to her now. So there were two buildings that hadn't changed, her beach house and the church. Two genuine places.

As she ran, she focused ahead, lost in her thoughts. But movement caught her attention to her right, and she glanced over, seeing the biggest house she'd seen on the beach. One of the modern ones, the back of it was all glass. Her eyes were drawn upward where two people stood on the rooftop. She couldn't see their faces, but the shape of the guy looked familiar. Jared? What was he doing up there? He lifted his hand as if to wave, but the woman who had her arm around his waist waved too. So maybe he was attached to someone.

Disappointment coursed through her, putting a pall on the run. Why wouldn't he be? He was a good-looking, nice guy. Just because he hadn't gotten married didn't mean he wasn't in a relationship. The woman sure acted like they were a couple. But he had asked Courtney to lunch. Guess that didn't count as a date, just two old friends getting together. That was fine. All she wanted was a friend anyway. A handsome one didn't hurt either.

She turned around to go back to the house, hoping she wouldn't see Jared and his "friend" again. She averted her gaze as she neared the mansion and thankfully, saw no one. Reaching her place, she used the outside hose to rinse off her feet and Tucker's. "Boy, I need to bathe you." But his bath would have to wait because fatigue was settling in. Feeling as if she were being watched, she glanced at the house next door. A man and woman sat on their back deck, staring at her.

"Hello!" Courtney waved and smiled.

They nodded but didn't smile. "That dog got a permit?" the man said.

A permit?

"Excuse me?" Courtney responded.

"A permit. You're supposed to have one if you have a dog on the beach. County law."

"Oh, I'm sorry. I didn't know. This is only my second day here."

"Well, you better get a permit, or the county will pick up that dog."

What? Would they really do that?

She forced a polite smile. "Thank you for telling me. I'll take care of that first thing tomorrow." Nice to meet you, too.

She brushed the sand off Tucker's thick fur before they went back into the house. How was she supposed to know about a permit? How long had that law been around? So that explained some of the dirty looks she'd gotten on the beach. She needed to ask Jared what to do, how to get the permit. She sure didn't want any trouble over Tucker.

What was his number? She looked through the kitchen drawers for a list of numbers but didn't find one. Remembering the stack of business cards on the counter, she riffled through them. Was his included? No, he didn't give her a card. What was the name on his shirt? She visualized the shirt stretched across Jared's chest. Coastal Real Estate, that was it. She could call them tomorrow. Too bad she didn't have his cell phone. Since they were friends, wouldn't it be okay to call him when he wasn't working? No, she shouldn't assume too much. Not to mention the fact that he appeared to be busy with *other* things after work.

Meanwhile, she wanted to enjoy the beach view from her porch. She wasn't very hungry, so grabbed a bunch of grapes, Havarti cheese and some crackers to munch on. A glass of chardonnay would be nice too, if she had any. For now, water was sufficient. Sitting out on the screened porch, she compared it to the decks and porches she'd seen on the other houses. Nobody had screened porches anymore. She would certainly have a better view of the water if the screen wasn't there, and the porch was open. But then other people would have a better view of her too. There was something to be said about "hiding" on the porch. From her secret perch, she could watch her neighbors on their deck. Her unfriendly neighbors. The man could have certainly been more polite when he spoke to her.

Looked like they weren't the chummy type anyway. Guess she wouldn't be invited over for dinner. She was okay with that. She'd wanted to be alone anyway, hadn't she? She opened her phone to social media and began checking what her "friends" were doing on Facebook and Instagram. Going to parties, weddings, baby showers. Everyone's life looked perfect, like it was following the planned order it was supposed to—parties, weddings, babies. Somehow, she'd missed the boat for those things. In marketing, they'd used the term "window of opportunity." Courtney thought she'd missed hers, as far as the plan went. Looked like she better take up a hobby. With her job out of the picture and no friends to hang out with, she'd have to find something else to occupy her time.

Painting? Not talented enough. Writing? Only marketing copy. Needlework? Boring. Reading? Well, she already did that. Did it count as a hobby? She did her yoga everyday too, but only for an hour. Surfing? No waves, besides, she didn't care to battle sharks. Skydiving? Didn't have the guts. Kayaking? Now, that was a possibility, but not here in the Gulf. Was there a place near here she could kayak? As if on cue, a woman on a paddleboard paddled by in the calm waves. That looked like something she could do. Where could she get one?

That was another question to ask Jared. She hated to bother him, but she was thankful she had *someone* to ask, the only person so far who had been friendly. She exhaled a long sigh. Tucker came over and put his paw on her lap. Courtney leaned down and hugged the dog's head. "Well, at least I have you for a friend. You won't leave me, will you?" Tucker licked her face. How could someone not like Tucker? He was the nicest dog ever.

~

"Do I smell gumbo?" The aroma of his mom's specialty and Jared's favorite food greeted him as he walked into the kitchen of his parents' house.

"Sure is." His mother smiled a greeting as she stirred a pot on the stove. "It's been a long time since I made it for you."

Jared leaned over and gave her a kiss on the cheek. "You spoil me, Mom."

"She tries to spoil both of us." Dad sat on a stool with his elbows resting on the large island that separated the kitchen from the living room. Jared went over to him and placed his arm on his father's shoulder, giving it a slight squeeze.

"Well, I'm not complaining," Jared said. "Who else is going to do it?"

"We need to work on that," Mom said, glancing over her shoulder. "I'm sure there's some nice single girls at church."

Jared groaned. "Mom, I'm a little too old for *girls*."

She swatted him with the dish towel. "You know what I mean. Will you come to church with us this week, now that you're back from duty?"

"Sure, Mom. If it'll make you happy." He gave her a wink as he dodged the towel.

"Guess I'll have to settle for that reason, although I hope you'd go to church for yourself as well."

"Can't I do both?"

"Of course, dear." Mom pointed to a stack of dishes. "Everything's ready. Rice, gumbo, salad and French bread. Help yourself. I thought we'd eat on the patio since it's a nice temperature outside tonight. Would you like some tea?"

"Yes, ma'am. You did raise a southern boy, you know."

"I'll carry the salad out there. The table's already set with silverware and napkins. Jared, will you please bring the bread?"

He nodded and picked up the basket of bread. "Yes, ma'am."

"What can I do, Lisa?" Dad slowly stood from the stool.

"David Freeman, you can just go on out and sit down at the table. I'll bring you your food."

Dad shook his head. "She won't let me do anything."

"Hey, Dad. Take advantage of this royal treatment. She might hand you a honey-do list next." Jared smiled, trying not to let his face show his concern for his father. Dad looked weak, and his skin was pale, so unlike the tanned, robust man he used to be.

"Can I at least have a beer?" Dad implored his wife.

"Oh, all right. I guess it won't hurt you."

"Gee, thanks." Dad grumbled.

Jared started to get it for his father but held back to let the man do something for himself, even if he was painstakingly slow. His father took the beer bottle from the refrigerator, and Jared reached out for it. Without a word, Dad handed it over so Jared could open it for him, then Jared handed it back. Dad went outside to the table on the stone patio surrounded by jungle foliage with a water feature trickling nearby. In the kitchen, Jared put some rice in a soup bowl and ladled some gumbo over it. He glanced up at his mother who waited for him so she could get his father's food. "Hot sauce is already on the table." She always could read his mind.

Once they were all seated, Dad blessed the food. Dipping his spoon into the hot mixture, Jared made sure he got some shrimp and sausage on the first spoonful. "Yum, Mom. Your gumbo is better than ever."

"You just haven't had it in a while but thank you anyway."

"So what did Merrilee want this time?" Dad asked.

Jared rolled his eyes. "She claimed her pool was leaking. Of course, she hadn't called a pool company to come check it."

"What did you do? Anything?"

"Pretended to check it out." Jared set down his spoon and picked up a piece of bread. "Really, Dad, the woman is such a pain. How have you put up with her so long?"

"She just wants attention, that's all. Her husband Stan gave us a lot of business, and he asked me to look after her, help her make real estate decisions."

"I think you've gone over and above that request."

"Now, Jared, I told you she's just a lonely woman. We have to be kind to her." Mom reminded him to look beyond the surface. But did Mom know how flirtatious the woman was? How a woman her own age came on to him?

He pursed his lips. "I try to be nice and polite, even when she's wasting my time."

"That's all we ask. Show her Christian love."

Jared didn't think that was the kind of love Merrilee wanted, but he kept his mouth shut so he wouldn't offend his mother.

Mom patted the table. "So tell me about Courtney Morgan! What's she doing now?"

"She said she went to work for a large corporation after she got her master's in marketing."

"That sounds impressive. And she's here by herself?"

"Yes, well, she has a dog, a pretty golden retriever."

"Those are nice dogs. Bless her heart, I remember how lanky Courtney was back then."

"She's not now. She really looks great." An image of her long legs running on the beach popped into his mind. "It was nice to catch up with her."

"Well, I'd love to see her. Wouldn't you, Dave?" Mom glanced at Dad for his nod of agreement. "Why don't you ask her over here for dinner?"

A tree frog nearby emitted a loud barking sound.

"That's a good idea, Mom." And a good excuse to see Courtney again." I'm sure she'd like to see you and Dad too. I'll ask her."

"Good." Mom put her spoon down. "How are her parents?"

"Courtney says they travel all the time, so they must be doing fine."

"And her brother Clay? Where is he now?"

"Married with two kids in Colorado."

"Well, how nice. I'm glad to hear they're all doing well."

"Did she say anything about selling the beach house?" Dad asked, always in real estate agent mode.

Jared frowned. "No, Dad. We didn't discuss business."

"If nobody's gonna use that place anymore, they ought to sell it."

"I know. But at least someone is using it now."

"How long is she going to stay here?" Mom asked.

"She didn't say."

"I imagine the place needs some sprucing up," Mom said. "Goodness knows the last time it was cleaned."

"That's what she was doing when I stopped by. Other than needing cleaning and a little worn, it looks just like it always has."

"You mean, old," Dad said.

"Compared to everything else around here, yes, it does."

"Such a nice piece of property," Dad continued. "Somebody could put a nice home there."

"Well, if she comes to dinner here, you can talk to her about it."

"Oh, I hope she comes. I can't wait to see her again!" Mom's eyes sparkled.

Jared felt the same way.

Chapter Seven

The next morning Courtney called Jared's office, but he wasn't in, so she left a message with the receptionist. While she was having her coffee on the porch, she opened her iPad to see what might be going on in Serendipity. An ad for an art fair caught her attention. Checking the date, she discovered it began today. Perhaps it was time for her to see more of Serendipity besides the beach. Maybe she could meet some new friends too.

The downstairs was as clean as she could get it, but she planned to tackle the upstairs today. However, she could start on it this morning, then have time to go to the fair after lunch. In fact, maybe she could find a place to eat lunch while she was out. She glanced down at Tucker. "Sorry, boy, I better not bring you until you're legal, and I can find out if people are allowed to bring dogs to the fair."

Her phone buzzed, but she didn't recognize the number. Hopefully, it wasn't spam.

"Hello?" She half-expected a pause and then the sound of a room full of people in the background.

"Courtney, it's Jared. You called the office?"

"Yes, Jared." Warmth curled in her stomach like she'd taken a big sip of hot coffee. "My neighbors informed me that I need a permit for Tucker."

"That's true, one of the new rules around here, unfortunately. I was going to call you today and tell you about it, but I didn't have your number. But now I do. I saved it to my phone.

"Good. So this is your cellphone too?"

"Yes. Feel free to call anytime. Everybody else does," he said with a laugh.

"So how do I get a permit? Do I have to go somewhere to get it?"

"Yes and no. You can go to the county office in person, or you can go online, whichever you prefer. There's a fee of course, so however you want to pay might determine what you do."

"Where is the county office? I was planning to get out today, so I might have time to go by there."

"It's about five miles from here. Would you like me to take you?"

"No, I'm sure I can find it myself." The reply came automatically, her standard response to offers of help when her independence was threatened. But she immediately regretted her quick response to him. "I saw there's an art fair in town. Is it within walking distance from here?"

"Yes, it is, probably a couple of miles from your place. Parking's always scarce in town, so if you don't mind walking, you'd be better off."

"Fine. I don't mind walking. In fact, I did quite a bit of it when I lived in the city."

"You should probably drive to the county office though."

"Right. Actually, since I need to get this permit right away, maybe I'll just do it online. I'll get it instantly, won't I?"

"Yes, you can print it off and carry it with you." He paused. "Hey, why don't I meet you at the fair? It's near my office. We can grab lunch at the fair. How does that sound?"

It sounded great. But what about that woman on the rooftop with him? Would she mind? But then, she and Jared were just friends. She needed to keep reminding herself of that fact.

"Sounds good. Meet you at your office?"

"Sure. How about noon?"

"All right. Jared, do you know if dogs will be allowed at the fair? I'd bring Tucker if they are."

"I think so. I'll check it out and let you know beforehand. Just get that permit."

"Yes, sir, will do." She halted. "Oh, I just remembered I don't have a printer."

"Then let me do it for you. I can print it off at my office. Give me Tucker's info – type, I know, weight, vaccinations up to date?"

Courtney relayed all Tucker's information.

"Got it. I'm logging onto the website now." The sound of clicking on a keyboard came through the phone. As he filled in the blanks, he read the form out loud.

Courtney tapped her fingernails on the table while she waited.

"There! All done now. I'll just print this off and bring it with me."

"Wait. Isn't there a fee?"

"Yeah, no problem. I took care of it."

"But you shouldn't have to do that. Tell me what it is and I'll pay you back."

"That's not necessary."

"Jared. I want to." She didn't want to feel like she owed him anything.

"Okay, if you insist, you can buy my lunch."

"Is that all?"

He laughed. "You haven't seen how much I can eat!"

"All right. So do you think I should bring Tucker with me? What if I get stopped before I get the permit?"

"If that happens, just tell them I have it and you're coming to get it from me."

Courtney paused to consider that option. "Okay, if say so. I'll see you at noon."

After the call ended, Courtney finished her coffee and took the cleaning supplies upstairs. The second floor had two bedrooms on each side. One of the bedrooms was larger than the rest and had three sets of bunkbeds to accommodate all the kids. There were three bathrooms, one adjacent to the bunk room and one for the other bedroom, then one between the other two bedrooms across the hall. Courtney stripped all the beds and piled the linens in the hallway. She hoped the washer and dryer still worked. While she dusted off the furniture and windowsill, her thoughts drifted back to Jared, and a tingle of excitement coursed through her. She did look forward to seeing him again, if only to have some human companionship. Not that Tucker's companionship was bad—he was a good listener, but he wasn't much of a conversationalist.

When she finished the dusting, she tackled the bathrooms, then she swept all the floors. A glance at her fitness watch told her it was time to change to meet Jared. The rest would have to wait. She ran downstairs and jumped in the shower, then threw on a white tank top and tan linen shorts. Over the tank, she tied a loose-fitting, lightweight white shirt, tying it in front at the waist, then braided her hair in one long braid.

Since Tucker was going with her, she took him outside to let him do his business, then brush him. When they came back in, she found one of his bandanas, an aqua one, and tied it around his neck. "You need to look nice too, Tucker. We need to make a good impression." She slipped on her leather Birkenstocks, put on a straw hat with a black headband, and threw her small shoulder bag across her chest and shoulder. "Let's go see what's happening around here."

They trotted down the front steps, then navigated the broken walkway before turning onto the small neighborhood street. She passed several older cottages, similar in style to hers, but much smaller and not on the beach before the intersection with Main Street. She was glad to see other houses from the past that had remained. But in front of every one was a sign that read "Beach Rentals." Funny that although none of these houses were actually *on* the beach, they were within walking distance, so they could claim the title. At the intersection with the main street was a colorful sign with various business names on separate pieces of wood shaped like arrows. She turned right and headed down the street.

Along the way, she passed an Italian restaurant tucked away from the road, the name La Trattoria carved on the sign. The Mediterranean red tile roof and white facade designated the establishment as an upscale eatery. She also passed by a bohemian-style store boasting an orange exterior with purple shutters, and an assortment of yard art scattered in front of the business. Another house-turned-business was an art gallery. Strips of undeveloped land between the businesses provided the taste of old Florida, and the presence of trees standing in water meant the area was too swampy to build on. Thank God for that.

The closer she got to town, the more commercial it became, although still low-key and more artsy than modern. She looked for Smith's Trading Post, the place they used to go to for fishing tackle, bait, beach toys, and ice cream. Back in the day, it was the only place that had a gasoline pump. But Smith's was gone, and in its place was a new convenience store, the sign street-level and the property surrounded by palm trees in an attempt to blend in with the locale. After a few more blocks, she spotted the sign for Coastal Real Estate in front of a white-washed brick building with black shutters that looked like it had formerly been a residence. A healthy sago palm filled the small yard space between the sidewalk and the house.

Jared trotted down the front steps with a wide grin that made her smile back. "Hello, Courtney! You look great!" Glancing at Tucker, he said, "You look nice too, Tucker, all dressed up with your bandana!" Tucker wagged his tail in appreciation.

He pulled a folded piece of paper from his pocket and handed it to her. "Here you go. Tucker's legal now."

"Thank you, Jared, that was really nice of you."

"Not a problem." He glanced around. "Are you hungry?"

"Famished. I worked up quite an appetite this morning."

"Then let's go." He took her free hand and led her across the street. They walked another block before the space opened up to a large green space around which was a horseshoe shaped drive. On one side of the drive a row of identical little cottages in a rainbow of colors lined up. In the grassy area was an assortment of tents and canopies under which vendors displayed their wares. A small stage under a large floating canopy had musicians setting up. Three food trucks parked near the road advertised tacos, po'boys, or Cuban sandwiches.

"What kind of food are you in the mood for? Besides the food trucks, there are two cafes in the cottages, one sells wraps and salads and the other has Thai bowls."

"Hmm. It all sounds good, but I think I'd prefer wraps and salads right now."

Courtney was relieved to see other people with their dogs. Some were little fluffy dogs like Bichons and Shih Tzus, but there was also a lab, a goldendoodle and a Great Dane. Tucker whined a little, but he and the other dogs were well-mannered and didn't create a problem.

"I'm glad to see so many dogs," she said. "I

don't feel like I'm standing out with Tucker."

"See? There are some nice people here." Jared gave her a wink.

"Is there a dog park near here? I used to take Tucker to one so he could mingle with other dogs."

"There's been talk of one, but no one wants to give up their property for a dog park. If we had one, it would probably be run by the county, and they don't have the extra land."

They moseyed over to the row of colorful cottages, all trimmed in white with white steps leading to the front door. The first one in the row, Art on the Beach, a local art gallery, was blue. Beside it was Java Jane's, a coffee shop. On the side of the yellow cottage a porch with small tables and chairs ran the length of the building, was particularly inviting. It would be a cool place to meet friends for coffee, if she had any here. Next to Java Jane's was a pink building featuring a glass artist. And beside the coffee shop was a lime green building, Serendipity Bread Company, whose sign boasted homemade bread and muffins. The aroma wafting from the shop was enticing, and blending with the coffee scent from Java Jane's, made Courtney's mouth water.

"You will get hooked on that place," Jared said, as they passed the bread store. "Their bread and muffins are out of this world."

"Sounds like it could become a weakness. I love fresh bread." Her stomach growled in agreement.

Next to the bread store was a lavender cottage, the Sea Oats Craft Bar, featuring specialty beers. Courtney and Jared's destination was next, a peach-colored cottage whose sign read "It's a Wrap." They stepped up to the front window and placed their order, then poured their own beverages from the self-service dispensers, Jared choosing strawberry lemonade and Courtney selecting raspberry-pomegranate tea. Walking around to the side porch, they found a table for two. They set down their drinks and claimed the chairs beneath the blue-and-peach-striped umbrella. Tucker plopped down on the painted white deck, enjoying a spot in the shade.

"What a perfect day for this event," Courtney said. "I'm really enjoying it."

"Good to hear," Jared said. "Even though things have changed, they're not all for the worst. The town has tried to maintain its identity as a quaint beach village. You'll notice there are no buildings taller than one story, and any new building has to add Florida-style greenery like palms. Large lighted signs aren't permitted, and all signs have to be at street level, visible only by cars or pedestrians."

"I'm glad. But some of the houses on the beach seem to violate those rules." Her mind flashed to the three-story house where she saw Jared.

Grimacing, he replied. "The beach is another thing altogether. Money talks big over there, and people have more freedom to build what they want."

"There was one house in particular that stood out. It was much larger than the rest and more contemporary too." Should she tell him she saw him there on the rooftop? With a woman?

"I know which one you mean. There's a long

story about that one."

What was the story about the woman? Never mind, it wasn't her business.

"Don't you find it ironic that there's freedom about building, but not freedom to enjoy the beach?"

He arched a brow. "What do you mean?"

"All those 'no trespassing' signs! Remember how we used to go wherever we wanted to on the beach? What's happened to people?"

He smiled, then spread out his hands. "And we thought *we* owned the beach! But these days, people that pay so much for their beachfront property, they think they're the only ones entitled to use it."

"What happened to sharing?" She flipped her braid over her shoulder.

"Sharing is more selective now, unfortunately."

Courtney shook her head. "That's too bad."

Chapter Eight

Man, she was gorgeous. With her hair in a braid and that cute straw hat perched on her head, Courtney looked like a model. She certainly had the figure to be one. Moving with such grace, she was so unlike the lanky girl he remembered. Poise had replaced the teenage awkwardness with a calming effect that was soothing to be near. The spring breeze played with loose strands of her long hair, giving Jared the urge to do so as well.

When she asked him about Merrilee's house, she fixed him with a look that asked a question, although none was asked. Had she recognized him on the rooftop? He wanted to explain, but Merrilee's arm around his waist complicated matters. And if she was so irritated about the trespassing signs, he couldn't imagine her response to Merrilee, who was as fake as Courtney was genuine.

Their number was called, so Jared went to pick it up. As he was carrying the tray back with their food, he spotted Merrilee. He hoped she didn't see him. Setting the food down on the table, he said, "Dinner—that is, lunch—is served, mademoiselle."

"Merci," Courtney said. She eyed the tomato

stuffed with chicken salad that she ordered, a garnish of sliced avocado and mango on the side. "This looks great."

"You won't be disappointed." Jared's plate held a large turkey-bacon wrap cut in half with a side of homemade potato chips and a pickle spear. He picked up a potato chip and showed it to Courtney. "You really should try these."

She snatched it from his hand and put it in her mouth. "Yum! These are good!"

He motioned to his plate. "Take as many as you'd like."

Jared had just taken a bite of his wrap when a hand landed on his shoulder.

"There you are, Jared! I've been looking all over for you, honey."

He almost choked at the sound of Merrilee's voice. He grabbed his drink to swallow down his food before looking up.

She stood beside their table holding Sweet Pea wearing a pink bow on her head and a jeweled collar around her neck. Merrilee, lips slathered in red lipstick, wore some kind of thin, flowery loose blouse over a red tank top that did little to hide her cleavage and some kind of loose pants that looked like pajamas and matched the flowery top. He cringed, and a wave of perspiration popped out on his forehead. He glanced at Courtney for her reaction. She angled her head to look at Merrilee from under her hat, then turned to him with a questioning look.

Jared swallowed hard, then remembering his manners, started to stand up. Merrilee's hand pressed down on his shoulder.

"Oh, don't bother getting up, Jared. Enjoy your lunch." Merrilee grinned and focused on Courtney. "I don't believe we've met. I'm Merrilee Chambers."

Jared recovered his voice. "Merrilee is one of our clients."

"Oh, don't let him fool you. I'm much more than a client. I'm a very close friend."

Jared hated the way she inferred something immoral. He glanced at Courtney and rolled his eyes, hoping Merrilee didn't see his gesture.

Courtney extended her hand. "I'm Courtney Morgan. Jared and I have been friends a long time."

Sweet Pea growled, and Tucker sat up, eyeing the little dog he could snap in two if he had a mind to.

Merrilee's eyes narrowed before her fake smile reappeared. "Oh, I see. And are you visiting someone here?"

"No, actually, I'm staying in our family's beach house for a while."

A tiny frown attempted its way past the Botox between Merrilee's eyes. "Oh? Which house is that?"

"It's the retro beach house, you know, the white frame one with the screened-in porch."

Merrilee's eyes rounded. "Oh, you don't mean that old ramshackle thing? Well, bless your heart! I'm surprised it hasn't fallen down by now."

Jared cleared his throat. "Actually, Merrilee, it's very solidly built."

She cut a glare toward him. "Hmm. Well, I'm

sure it must be ancient inside. How long has it been since anyone has been there? I don't remember ever seeing anyone there."

"Actually, Merrilee, you might not have lived here then. It's been about ten years."

"My grandfather built it, and our family used to spend summers here when I was a child. But we've all grown up and gone our separate ways, so unfortunately, no one has been here for a while. It just needed a good cleaning, which is what I've been doing."

Her lips curled into a smile, Merrilee said, "Why bother? Why not just sell the old thing and get it off your hands? I'm sure you could make a pretty penny on it, even in its sad condition."

Courtney's eyes darkened, and her lips tightened. "My family has no intention of selling it."

"Well, I hope it's safe. You know, it's probably breaking all the building codes."

"The house is grandfathered in, Merrilee, so it's exempt from the codes." Jared intervened in Merrilee's negative attack.

"Now that hardly seems right, does it? I mean, everyone else has to abide by the codes. I know when they built my house, they strictly went by the book."

"Oh, and your house is?"

Merrilee blew out an exaggerated breath. "You don't know? Oh, I guess you wouldn't, being a newcomer and all. My house is the biggest one on the beach. It has three stories and is very modern."

"Oh, yes, I remember seeing it when I ran down

the beach yesterday."

"So that was you?" Merrilee looked from Courtney to Tucker. "Now I remember. I noticed the dog wasn't on a leash. Did you know you're supposed to have a permit for the dog on the beach?"

Courtney smiled. "Yes, of course. Tucker has one." She glanced at Jared. "Jared took care of that for me." Tucker stood at the sound of his name, wagging his tail.

Sweet Pea barked at Tucker as Merrilee's face reddened. "Well how nice of him." She fanned herself with her free hand. "I simply must get something to drink."

"Can I get you a lemonade, Merrilee?" Jared felt obligated to offer, if only to quell the tension.

Merrilee laughed. "No, thank you, sweetheart. I need an adult beverage." She glanced over her shoulder. "I'll just mosey over to the cocktail tent." Returning her gaze to Courtney, she offered a fake smile. "It's been nice talking to you, dear. You take care in that old house. I hope it doesn't have rats in it, being empty so long and all."

"Oh, it doesn't anymore. Tucker caught them all." Courtney returned a fake smile.

Merrilee huffed. "I'll be talking to you later, Jared." She spun and sashayed away.

Jared burst out laughing and Courtney joined him. "I can't believe you told her Tucker caught the rats in the house!"

"I couldn't help myself. She was trying so hard to freak me out about the house."

"Hey, I'm sorry about all that. Merrilee likes to

lord over everyone that she has the biggest, nicest house on the beach."

"Biggest maybe, but I disagree with nicest. I don't like its style and wouldn't trade ours for hers if you paid me."

"It's not my favorite style either, but her husband wanted to give her everything she asked for."

"Where is he now? Did they get divorced?"

Jared shook his head. "No, he was quite a few years older than her, and not in great health. He passed away a couple of years ago, but he was good friends with my father and asked Dad to take care of her real estate investments after he died."

"She has other property?"

"Yes, there are quite a few properties she inherited, mostly commercial. We take care of the rental of the properties for her."

"So I *did* see you on her rooftop. I thought that was you."

"Yes, that was me. I had to go check out some problem she supposedly had. Dad used to handle all her issues, but his health doesn't allow him to give her much attention anymore."

"And the responsibility is on you now."

Jared shrugged. "More or less. Dad still knows what's going on, in case I need his advice." They finished eating their lunch, and Jared gathered their trash to clear the table. "Shall we explore the festival?"

"Yes, please. Thank you for suggesting this place. The food is really good."

"Sure. We can do lunch here again someday."

He snapped his fingers. "I almost forgot. Mom wanted me to ask you to come over to the house for dinner tonight. It may be late notice, but if you don't have any other plans…"

"I don't, and I'd love to see your parents. I'll have to walk off this lunch before I can eat again, though."

"Great. I'll call her and let her know right now. I can't text her because she never knows when she has a text."

Chapter Nine

So, the mystery woman was revealed. Courtney didn't know why she was relieved to find out who Merrilee was, but the knowledge felt like a burden lifted. Poor woman. She'd obviously spent a lot of money to look younger, but the end result was an abnormal appearance. One thing Courtney admired about her own mother was how she embraced her age with grace, saying she was thankful for the years she'd lived. "To be a classic, you have to have some years behind you, so I'm classic, not old," was one of Mom's favorite expressions.

And how weird that Merrilee was obviously jealous of Courtney. The woman was old enough to be Jared's mother, however, she still wanted attention, even if she did go the wrong way about getting it. Courtney couldn't argue that Jared was a good-looking guy, though, and any woman any age could appreciate that fact. Whether it was his military training or something else, he was in great shape, evidenced by the way his shirt stretched over taut chest muscles and biceps. She was still amazed that this guy was the one she'd called "Shrimp."

Jared really was a nice guy too—well-mannered and polite to Merrilee, even though he didn't seem happy about her showing up. Courtney observed him as he spoke to his mother on the phone and was close enough to hear the conversation. He nodded and smiled, glancing at Courtney a couple of times and winking. A warm sensation coursed through her, making her face flush. She turned away to check out the activities around them, but in reality, trying to calm down the feelings that he'd stirred.

"All right, Mom. I'll tell her. See you later."

Courtney faced him again, after he disconnected the call.

"She wanted me to tell you to bring Tucker. She loves dogs, especially goldens. We had one several years ago."

"Really? Well, if it's okay with her, I'll bring him." She looked down at her dog. "He's well-behaved." Glancing back up at him, she said, "Thank you again for taking care of the permit. I'm glad I could tell Merrilee I had one."

"Not a problem. I don't think her dog liked Tucker very much."

Courtney laughed and looked back down at Tucker. "Tucker doesn't care. He's got good self-esteem." Tucker wagged his tail, knowing he was being talked about.

They strolled through the various tents displaying handmade jewelry, quilted beach totes and gauzy beach dresses. At one of the tents, Courtney picked up some lemongrass soap and sniffed it. "I love this scent. I have to get some." On the way to pay for it, she spotted some candles in jars and test-sniffed several of those. One was a coconut-lime scent, so she decided to buy it too. "The house could use a nice fresh smell."

Courtney paused at the art displays to admire the seaside themes. There was a pair of vertical paintings of herons she considered buying. They'd certainly brighten up the beach house. She studied them, trying to figure out where they'd look best.

"Are you going to buy those?" Jared asked. "They're nice. This guy does good work."

"I'm not sure if I should buy them now. I think the walls might need to be repainted before I hang any new pictures."

"I can help with that."

"You can? I thought you hired people to do things like that."

"I do, if it's too complicated or the ceiling is too high."

"Actually, one of the walls is pretty high." She faced him. "What did Merrilee mean about building codes? Is there a chance my house doesn't meet the codes? What should I do about it? Should I be worried?"

"No, like I told Merrilee, the house is grandfathered in, which makes it exempt from current codes. However, if you want to make any renovations, they'll have to comply with the codes."

They completed their tour of the grounds and stopped to watch the small jazz combo play. To their left, Merrilee danced with, or rather around, a gentleman whose imbalance denoted too much time in the cocktail tent, which he had in common with his dance partner.

Jared shook his head. "Poor Merrilee."

"What do you mean? She seems to be having a good time."

"Yes, she does. She just seems so …"

"Needy?" Courtney finished his thought.

He glanced at her and nodded. "Yes, exactly. I wish she could find someone to settle down with. My mother says Merrilee is a lonely woman and needs to go to church to meet other women friends. But Merrilee spends her time and money trying to attract men."

"I see what you mean." Courtney faced Jared. "Does your family still attend that little church in town?"

"Yes, they're part of the church's foundation, you know, and feel obligated to stay there, even though there are larger churches in the area that attract most people these days."

"I've been to those too, when I was in the city. But they just don't have the feel of a small community church. I think I'll go Sunday. What time is the service?"

"Eleven o'clock. Would you like me to come get you?"

"No, thank you. I'll just see you there." She glanced over at Merrilee again, stumbling and laughing as she tried to dance. "I better get back to the house and clean up before dinner tonight."

"You look pretty clean to me," Jared said with a grin. "I'll pick you up at six o'clock. All right?"

"Perfect," she said.

~

On the walk home, the image of Merrilee came

to Courtney's mind. The woman had everything, material-wise—money, house on the beach, any clothes or jewelry she wanted and any plastic surgery she deemed necessary. But she wasn't happy because she was alone. What a shame that her husband had died. Would she ever find someone else, someone who truly loved her and not just for her money?

At least she'd been happy once before, and she'd been loved. Which was something Courtney couldn't claim for herself. Would she be a lonely old woman someday like Merrilee? The thought shook her. Of course, she wouldn't have the fortune to spend that Merrilee had, but what if she stayed at the beach house the rest of her life? Just she and Tucker, getting old like the house. What an awful thought! She loved the beach house, but she had to admit that now that she didn't have a job to think about, she felt the pangs of loneliness.

Jared had helped to appease some of that pain. She was so thankful to have reconnected with him and enjoy his friendship once again. But she hoped she didn't come across needy like Merrilee though. However, when it came to companionship, she'd rather have a good friend than forced relationships.

At the walkway that led to the front steps of the beach house, Courtney paused to give it a good look, remembering Merrilee's derogatory comments about the place. The house was partially hidden behind the overgrown bushes and huge magnolias that stood on either side. It could definitely use a fresh coat of paint. She had to agree, the house looked neglected and forgotten. Surely, she could do something about the condition. Did Grandpa have some pruning shears? She walked around to the side of the house and saw a small outbuilding beside the house, almost hidden by a shrub growing beside it. There was a lock on the door. Where on earth was the key?

She continued making a walk around the house, noticing other things that needed to be done. Some of the shutters were crooked, and one of the window screens had a tear. No wonder her neighbors disliked the house so much. She returned to the front of the house, and as she walked the sidewalk toward the front steps, she tripped and almost fell. Regaining her balance, she looked down. She had tripped on that broken, unlevel walkway more than once already.

When she went inside, she opened her iPad and created a to-do list of things the house needed. The more she looked around the house, the more things she saw that needed doing. How much could she do herself? And how long would it take to do them? Maybe, stretched out over a long period of time, they would get done, but meanwhile, where would she be? Eventually, her money would run out and she'd have to find a job and relocate. She closed the iPad and sighed. She hadn't bargained for a full-scale renovation.

A knock sounded at the door. She checked the time on her watch. It was too early for Jared. Whoever it was knocked again, and Tucker started barking.

"Shhh, Tucker! Quiet!"

She crossed to the door and opened it to find a

forty-ish professional-looking woman in a gray pencil skirt and a white short-sleeve top. The woman's black hair was cut in a swing bob, and her make-up was perfectly applied. She offered a wide grin that revealed unbelievably white teeth and extended her hand.

"Hi! I'm Jennifer Clark, and I'm with Beachfront Realty. I understand you're the owner of this property?"

"My family is. What can I do for you, Jennifer?" As if she didn't know.

"Call me Jen. I heard you might be interested in selling the property, and I'd love to help you with that."

"Jen, I don't know where you heard that, but we're not interested in selling."

Jen's brow creased and she cocked her head at an angle. "You're not? Hmm. Well, I supposed my source was wrong. But if you change your mind, please give me a call." She handed Courtney a business card.

"Thank you," Courtney started to close the door, then paused. "By the way, who told you we wanted to sell?"

"Merrilee Chambers. She knows everything that goes on around here." Jen smiled again.

Courtney offered a polite smile, then closed the door as Jen left. Leaning against the door, she blew out a breath. So Merrilee was spreading rumors about her selling the house? Just who did she think she was? Either she really hated the house or really wanted to get rid of Courtney. Her temper flared. She was sick of people trying to force her to do something she didn't want to do. Of course, that's what got her here in the first place. The bitter memory rose to the surface again, and her stomach tightened.

She needed to get in a quick run before getting ready for dinner. Running had always helped to clear her mind and remove stress. She quickly changed into a pair of running shorts, T-shirt and running shoes. She glanced at Tucker who was chilling on the tile floor of the kitchen. He'd walked enough today, so she'd leave him here this time. She scurried down the back steps, noticing again how uneven they were.

Her neighbor was sitting out on his deck again and saw her.

"You better get those steps fixed before someone falls and sues you." Was this man always watching her to find something she'd done wrong?

Courtney stopped at the bottom of the steps and studied them. Years of beach weather had taken its toll on them.

"They're probably not up to code. You don't have a hand railing and the steps are steeper than they should be."

Who was this guy, the building inspector?

She waved and forced a smile. "Thank you."

And then she ran. She'd come to this place for peace, but it seemed people were trying to take that peace away from her. Were all the homeowners on the beach watching her right now and talking to each other about her and her old beach house? She fought the urge to scan the houses and see. But she shouldn't be the one dealing with these issues, even though she was the only family member there. A call to her father would help. She'd call him after dinner.

Dinner! She needed to get back and get ready.

Chapter Ten

When Courtney opened the door for him, Jared was speechless. He didn't think she could be any more attractive, but she was. She wore a blue and yellow striped sundress and revealed enough of her cream skin to make him want to run his fingers over it. Her hair fell down her back in loose curls, and she was at least three inches taller, almost eye level with him. He looked down at her feet and discovered the reason, the espadrille wedges she wore.

"Ha! I thought you looked taller!"

She smiled and tilted her head in a teasing way. "Does my height still intimidate you, Jared?"

He drew himself up straight and lifted his chin. "Nope, not anymore. I've still got you by at least three inches."

She ran her hand from the top of her head to his mouth. "I guess you are taller. Who would've guessed back then?"

"I just had to grow to catch up with you." Jared winked. "So are you ready to leave?"

"Sure am. Are you sure I should take Tucker?"

"Absolutely. He's been invited too, and Mom will be disappointed if he doesn't come."

When they arrived at the home of his parents, Jared helped Courtney and Tucker out of the car, and together they walked up the newly pavered driveway to the front door. People thought it was odd that the Freemans didn't live on the beach. Being in the real estate business so many years, they'd had ample opportunity. But Jared's mother was afraid of hurricanes and didn't want to be so close to the water. Of course, if a really strong hurricane hit the coast near them, any house within five miles of the beach, including theirs, would suffer damage. It was a gamble beach lovers were willing to take, knowing the odds were pretty low they'd get a direct hit. As a result, the cost of insurance increased anytime a hurricane hit anywhere in the state of Florida. Or the insurance companies dropped the homeowner's policy altogether.

Jared tapped on the door, then opened it and called out. "We're here!"

Jared's mom answered. "Coming!"

They stepped inside the foyer as Mom hurried toward them.

"Oh, Courtney, you're beautiful!" She threw her arms around Courtney and hugged. "I'm so happy to see you again!" Mom leaned over to Tucker. "And this must be Tucker! What a pretty dog you are!" Tucker wagged his tail as Mom petted him. She grabbed Courtney's hand. "Come on out to the patio. David is looking forward to seeing you!"

Courtney glanced over her shoulder at him as

his mother led her through the house to the patio, Tucker following and Jared bringing up the rear.

Dad stood and hugged Courtney. "Courtney. So good to see you." He motioned to a chair. "Have a seat."

Jared took a seat as well while his parents fawned over Courtney. Like a fly on the wall, he watched as Courtney was the center of attention. They grilled her with questions about her family and what she'd been doing since they last saw her.

Mom got up to get the food from the kitchen and Jared went to help.

"Jared, she's just darling! Why didn't you tell me?"

"I thought I mentioned that she'd changed."

Mom gave him the look. "Changed, Jared? You must find her attractive. Don't you?"

Jared fought to keep cool and not let his mother see his reaction. He focused on putting ice in glasses. "Of course, I do. Who wouldn't?" He returned to the patio with the glasses, then returned to the kitchen for a pitcher of tea and a pitcher of water. Dad was enjoying his conversation with Courtney.

Mom carried a platter of salmon. "Would you get the asparagus and the wild rice, Jared?"

Jared returned with the rest of the food as requested.

"I hope you like salmon, Courtney," Mom said.

"I love it." Courtney's sweet smile could melt anyone's heart.

Dad said grace and thanked God for bringing Courtney back to the area. Jared said a silent 'amen' to that prayer.

"So, Courtney, do you think your parents are ready to sell the old house?" Dad said as he speared a piece of asparagus.

Courtney's expression changed, and a frown creased her brow. "We haven't talked about it, but I don't think so."

"You know, I don't understand why he lets it sit there without doing anything with it. He's sitting on a gold mine, you know."

"I think he wants to see if Clay or I want it." Her voice had tightened slightly, though remained polite.

"Hmm. I suppose so." Dad didn't seem to notice Courtney's reactions to this line of conversation. "But if no one's going to use it, why not sell it?"

Jared wished his father would abandon the topic and offered a reprieve. "Well, Courtney's using it now, aren't you, Courtney?"

Her shoulders relaxed, and she shot him an appreciative little smile. "Yes, I am."

"How long will you be here, Courtney?" Mom asked.

"I don't know yet."

"You don't have to get back to work?" Dad asked, fork midair.

"Not yet. I'm actually between jobs, so I'm enjoying some R and R."

"Well, I hope you stay a while. You're a welcome sight to us, a reminder of happier times," Mom said.

"I can't believe how much things have changed here," Courtney said. "I've been looking for the old places, but don't see many. I noticed Smith's Trading Post is gone."

"Actually, they moved the old building to another location. It's a seafood restaurant now. Pretty good one, too." Dad said.

"Remember how we used to hang out there when we weren't at the beach?" Jared said.

"I do. We had such fun. They had the best hamburgers and fries!" Courtney said.

"Not to mention ping pong, pool and a juke box."

"I believe I was the local pool champion," Courtney said, with a grin.

"You were the only one tall enough to reach across the table!" Jared said.

"You're probably right about that," Courtney said.

"I think we should have a rematch. I bet I could beat you now," Jared said.

"You're on. But where can you play pool around here?"

"Merrilee's house," Dad said. His comment was like dropping a bomb on the conversation. "Have you met her?"

"We met at the festival today." Courtney glanced from his dad to Jared, the lightness completely gone from her voice. "Why does it not surprise me that she has a pool table? It seems the woman has everything."

"Her late husband made the game room for himself, the only thing he claimed that was made just for him and not her."

"Speaking of Merrilee, she's telling people

we're selling the house. A real estate agent came by today to inquire about it. She said Merrilee told her we were selling."

Dad pointed his knife. "You tell any of those agents that contact you that if you do decide to sell, my company will handle it. After all, we've been overseeing it all these years."

Once again, Jared felt the need to rescue Courtney. "So, Courtney, I see you're still running. There's a race coming up pretty soon. If you're still in town, would you like to run it with me?"

Her expression showed interest. "How long is it?"

"There's a 5k and a 10k. What do you think?"

"Sure, I'd love to. I've run a few half-marathons, so that sounds like fun."

"You've run half-marathons? My, that's a long way," Mom said.

"Yes, ma'am. But I ran track in high school, so it's not a big deal."

Their meal finished, Mom stood to remove the plates and Courtney stood to help her.

"Now you're our guest. You don't need to do that," Mom chided.

"Please let me do something. I don't feel comfortable with you waiting on me."

Mom shrugged. "If you insist. You can bring out the dessert. I made a key lime pie."

"My favorite," Courtney picked up the serving dishes and followed his mother to the kitchen.

"Mom makes the best too. None of the restaurants make it as good as she does."

After they returned to the table and served the

pie, Courtney took a bite. "Oh my gosh. This is incredible!"

"Thank you," Mom said.

"I would like some advice from you, Mr. Freeman. The back steps off our porch need to be replaced. My neighbor said they don't meet code, plus they're in bad shape. Can you help me get them fixed and make them comply with the code?"

"Absolutely. Shouldn't be a problem. Jared, call Hank and get him out there." Jared nodded and Dad continued. "Hank does a lot of remodeling jobs for us."

"My neighbor said they need a railing too."

Dad nodded. "Yep, sure do. More than three steps, you need a handrail."

"Do you know what it will cost? I'll need to let my father know."

"Oh, probably a couple hundred or three."

"I noticed a few other things that need to be fixed too, like the shrubbery out front. There's a little shed of some type on the side of the house that might have some gardening tools, but it's locked, and I don't know where the key is. But maybe Daddy knows."

"We can always cut the lock for you. And if you don't find any pruning shears, we have some you can borrow. Or I can send out a landscaper to take care of that for you."

"You know, I want to do it myself. If there's something I can't do, I'll ask for help."

"I'll help you whether you ask or not," Jared said. Dad and Mom exchanged glances.

"The place will certainly look better with all that

cut back," Dad said.

"And let more daylight in. It's a little dark inside right now."

Jared rubbed his hands together. "Just put me to work!"

Courtney thanked him with a smile that would give him enough motivation to repair her whole house, is that's what she wanted.

Chapter Eleven

Jared showed up the next morning with wire-cutters and pruners.

"Will work for coffee!" he said with a grin.

A tremor of excitement coursed through Courtney at the sight of him. What a great way to begin her morning. Actually, she'd been up two hours, rising with the sun, and had already gotten a run in before anyone else was on the beach. After returning, she'd done some job searching on her laptop. There were several positions available in various cities across the country for which she was qualified, but she held off from submitting an application. At the moment, she didn't look forward to going anywhere, much less living there. Of course, she couldn't stay jobless. Becoming homeless and moving in with her parents was not an option. Still, she had a sensation like a hand on her shoulder telling her to wait. Was that God?

She held the door open for him. "Come on in. I'll get you a cup."

Brewing his cup and putting hers in the microwave to reheat, she said, "It was great seeing your parents again."

"They were beyond excited to see you too."

She handed him his cup. "How is your dad really doing? He's a lot thinner than I remember him."

"He's in remission, but the treatment really weakened him, plus made him lose his appetite." He took a sip of coffee. "I know he doesn't look good. I was shocked when I first laid eyes on him when I returned. But he's actually doing better now and has put on a few pounds."

"I'm glad to hear that." She glanced toward the back porch. "Would you like to go out there to drink your coffee?"

"Sure."

They headed out to the porch and sat down at the table.

"I've been thinking it might be nicer if the screen was removed from the porch, and we just had an open porch, kind of like the one next door. What do you think?"

"I think that's a great idea. You'd get a lot more breeze and be able to see the water better."

"I thought so too."

"But you know, Courtney, it sounds like you want to make several changes. Why not just sell the house as is and let the new buyer make whatever changes they want, that is, if they don't want to just start over."

Courtney cut him a glare. "Why do you keep talking about me selling the house? Is there some kind of conspiracy to get rid of me and my house?"

Jared's face registered shock, and he held up his hands. "No way, Courtney! The last thing I want to do is get rid of you." His face flushed. "And what you do with your property is not my business. I guess I was just talking like a real estate person, now that I've been indoctrinated into that world. I'm sorry."

"No, I'm sorry, Jared. I'm just so tired of people trying to get me to sell it." She mentioned all the phone calls and business cards she'd gotten. "I don't know how they got my phone number."

He looked sheepishly. "Maybe they called my office first to get your number."

"If that's the case, I'd appreciate it if your office would no longer give it out."

"I'll guarantee that happens." He took another swig of coffee. "Just curious, and please don't get angry, but do you plan to get the renovations done that you've mentioned while you're here? Because the porch might take a little while to get done."

She hadn't thought of that. "I don't really know. If I'm not here, then can your company make sure the job gets done right?"

He smiled and made a boy scout salute. "Yes, ma'am!"

"Then please contact someone to take care of the porch for me. Or can your guy, Hank?, do that too?"

"I'll check. Is there anything else you want to do? You also talked about painting. Have you picked out a color yet?"

"No, I've just thought about it."

"When you're ready, I can take you to the paint store."

"Jared, I appreciate your offers, but don't you

have other business to take care of?"

He shrugged. "I'm keeping an eye on things at the office. We all divide the work anyway, and our receptionist lets me know if there's something urgent." He glanced away.

"Is your father working any?"

"Not much. He just tries to find out what's going on and make sure we're taking care of his business. We try not to involve him in anything stressful."

"Do you think he plans to go back to work?"

Jared stared at the water. "I don't know. Mother's pushing him to retire permanently, but I worry that he needs something to keep busy."

"If he retires, does that leave you running the company?"

"I believe that's the plan." Hesitation hung on his flat tone as he kept he gaze on the water.

"Is that what you want to do?" She studied his reaction.

He shifted in his seat and exhaled a whoosh of air. "I believe the right question is, is that something God wants me to do? It had not been in my plans to come back here, but I believe God wanted me to. So I just have to trust him for the next step. Right?" He fixed his eyes on her.

"I understand. To be honest with you, I hadn't planned to be here now either."

His eyebrows lifted. "Tell me more."

Courtney sucked in a deep breath. Why not tell him what happened? She exhaled, then told him the whole ugly details of being let go from her job. Recounting the story was almost as bad as living through it. "So that's why I'm here. Regrouping, I guess."

Concern creased his brow and he shook his head. "Man, I'd like to punch that guy. What kind of creep does things like that?"

"A corporate creep. They're not all that rare, sadly. Power rules their choices."

"Then you're better off not working for him anymore." He studied her a moment. "I can tell it's really eating at you, though."

"Of course it is. But maybe you can't relate, since you're a man."

Jared drew back. "Hey, Courtney, remember me, your friend Jared?"

What was wrong with her? Why had she attacked him like that? "I'm sorry, Jared. That comment was uncalled for. I guess I still have a lot of anger about it."

"That's pretty obvious. Well, maybe you can relax while you're here and put that behind you."

"I hope so." She pointed her finger at Jared. "And don't ask me what I'm going to do next because I have no idea."

"Oh yeah? I know what you're going to do next." A grin tugged at his lips as he stood to his feet. Patting her hand, he said, "You're going to trim bushes. Let's get busy!"

They spent the next two hours trimming the bushes and trees back from the house. Sweat dripped down her back, and her ballcap did little to keep perspiration out of her eyes. Her back hurt from bending over so long, her arms tired, and her hands cramped from gripping the shears, but as she stepped back to assess their progress, she reveled in satisfaction at the work they'd accomplished.

Jared came over to stand beside her. "Looks a lot better already, doesn't it?"

She nodded, wiping her arm across her brow. "Definitely."

"Ready to knock off and get some lunch? I'm starving."

"Sure. What do you have in mind?"

"Pizza. There's an artsy pizza shack not too far from here. We can pick up or eat there."

"I don't think I'm presentable for public viewing."

His eyes fixed on hers. "You always look good. You've looked better, of course."

She gave him a shove, and he laughed.

"Beach Pizza has a deck right on the beach, so it's a great place to cool off."

"Okay, I'm game. Just let me wash off."

"All right. But don't change clothes. That wouldn't be fair."

"Fair?"

"If I can't change, you can't either."

A half hour later, Courtney sat on the deck, sated by the delicious pizza. They'd ordered one half vegetarian for her, and the other half loaded with meat for him. As Jared said, the sea breeze was wonderfully refreshing as they sat on the deck in the shade of a canopy.

"Now that the bushes are away from the house, it's obvious that the house needs to be painted." Her mind shifted away from food and back to work that needed to be accomplished.

"One thing leads to another. That's the beauty of home ownership, especially for older homes."

"I suppose I should wait on the painting until the porch is redone." She should start a priorities list. The number of repairs were growing.

"That would be a good idea."

"I'm going to call my dad later and get his opinion about things."

"Another good idea." He finished his piece of pizza and drank some cola. "Are you going to church tomorrow?"

"Tomorrow is Sunday, isn't it? Yes, I'd love to go."

"May I pick you up?"

She hesitated before answering. She didn't want to give the impression she had to be with him all the time. Finally, she said, "Okay. At least I'll know one person there."

"Three. Mom and Dad will be there too."

"Oh, good. It'll be kind of like old times."

"Except you and I won't be passing notes."

"Are you sure?" The childhood memory lit a spark in her chest. Jared must've felt it too, given the sparkle in his eye.

After they finished their pizza, Jared left to go clean up and head to his office.

Back at the beach house, Courtney opened her iPad and went to her to-do list. She checked off "trim the shrubs." She needed to talk to Dad about the rest of the list.

He answered after one ring. "Courtney? How are you?" She heard a muffled "It's Courtney," as he apparently covered the phone with his hand.

Nearby, her mom said, "Courtney? How is she? Put the phone on speaker."

Courtney rolled her eyes. "I'm fine."

"What have you been doing? Any leads on jobs?"

She didn't want to discuss jobs right now, so she told them about dinner with the Freemans and that they'd asked about her parents.

Before they could ask anything else, she said, "Dad, I'd like to get a few things done to the house while I'm here."

"Oh? I'm sure it needs some work, but how long will you be there?"

"Long enough. But Dad, I don't know how much things cost or if I should pay for them or if you want to."

"Tell me what you want to do."

Courtney explained about the steps and the porch, then the painting.

"Sounds more like a remodel."

"Sort of. But I understand some things aren't to code, like the steps, and even though nobody's going to make me fix them, if I do, they have to meet code."

"That sounds right. But why go to the trouble if no one's going to be there? It's been ten years since anyone has been, you know."

"Yes, I know. But I might want to start using the house more often."

"To tell you the truth, that place is your inheritance. It passed from my father to me, and it will pass to you and Clay. So it depends on what you two want to do with it."

"A lot of people are pressuring me to sell it." Courtney squirmed at the memory of the hungry-eyed agent who had stopped by the day before. "They say it's worth a lot of money, but they also say that whoever buys it will tear down the old house and build something new."

"That doesn't surprise me. I could've sold it by now, but I didn't need the money, and I was just waiting to see what you and your brother wanted to do."

"I don't want to sell it, Dad." The strength of passion in those words surprised Courtney. But it was true. This house was feeling like home. "I'll talk to Clay and see if he's okay with it. Why should he mind, when he hasn't been using it? And he's doing well and doesn't need the money either."

"You go ahead and talk to him. Meanwhile, get the repairs done and I'll pay for them. Let me know when you find out what they will cost."

"I will, Dad. Thanks! Love you!"

"We love you too, Courtney. Wait, what's that, honey? Mom says to tell you she's praying for you."

"Tell her thanks and give her a hug and a kiss for me. Bye!"

Chapter Twelve

The church was just as she'd remembered. Three sections of wooden pews faced the front, and behind the altar a stained glass of Jesus calming the sea was illuminated by sunlight.

Courtney counted about 75 people, meager compared to megachurch attendance, but in this little church, the number was just right. Ten people, four men and six women, occupied the choir loft in their street clothes instead of choir robes, one modern change that was evident. The music was a mix of contemporary praise and worship with a traditional hymn thrown in for good measure.

Courtney sat next to Jared who sat beside his parents. She stifled a chuckle, remembering scenes from the past and how their parents had to control their noise and try to make them focus on the minister. Courtney never knew what the minister had said, at least until she got to high school. There was a new minister now, and he preached on a Bible verse from Jeremiah, "For I know the plans I have for you, plans to prosper you and not to harm you, plans to give you a hope and a future."

She was glad to know God knew what he

wanted for her, but she'd appreciate it if He'd clue her in. She cut a sidelong glance at Jared, and he caught her eye and winked, sending warm fuzzies through her. The scene was so deja vu, as if time hadn't lapsed ten years and she was sitting with her family. Was it possible that God wanted her to be there?

As they were leaving church, one of the other church members walked over and introduced themselves.

"Howard Rosen. I hear Jared is handling the sale of your beach house." He glanced at Jared. Jared's face turned red, and he shook his head.

Courtney swallowed before answering. "You're mistaken. I'm not selling it."

Mr. Rosen's face had a confused expression. "Is that right? Hmm. Someone just told me that yesterday."

Courtney forced a polite smile. "Well, they're wrong."

Rosen leaned forward. "Can you tell me why not? I mean, you stand to make a good deal of money."

Courtney's temper flared, but she remembered where she was. "God told me not to sell it."

Rosen's eyebrows shot up and he laughed nervously. "That's a good one." He excused himself and hurried away.

Jared sputtered a laugh. "Seriously, Courtney? *God* told you?"

"How do you know He didn't?" She had made the comment as a joke, except the words sounded true. Was God telling her to stay?

~

On Monday, Hank showed up and checked out the steps and the porch.

"Yeah, I can do that. Me and my brother do a lot of remodeling around here, so we can do the porch too. It'll sure look a lot better without that old screen."

Hank gave her a quote for both jobs, and when Jared came over to take her to the paint store, she shared the figures with him.

"Sounds reasonable. Do you want another quote?"

"Not yet, I'll speak to my dad about it tonight."

Courtney chose a pale blue for the main room of the house. Jared estimated the size of the space they would paint, and she bought the appropriate amount.

When her father gave the go-ahead on Hank's estimate, Courtney called him the next day. For the next two weeks, work was going on at the beach house. Saws and hammers sounded outside during the day, while Jared came over each day for a couple of hours to help paint. Courtney was getting used to having him around and enjoyed the way they got along.

But it seemed that every time she went somewhere, she was told that Jared was selling her house. At the grocery store, she ran into a neighbor. At the nail salon, the woman doing her pedicure asked her in broken English. Was Merrilee the source for this rumor?

One day, Jared didn't come over, and Courtney's neighbor, Mr. Nosy-Pants, stood outside in his yard looking at the work being done on her house. "I guess Jared talked you into making these improvements, didn't he? He can get a better price for the place if it's spruced up and within code."

She wanted to give the man a snappy retort, but his reasoning niggled her with doubt about Jared. What if he really did plan to talk her into selling the house? What if he was encouraging all her improvements to help him sell the place? Did he ever actually deny the rumors? Maybe she shouldn't trust him so much. The more she thought about it, the more annoyed she became. Was he giving her so much attention with an ulterior motive? Didn't he say something about his father's company, soon to be *his* company, expected to have the right to sell the house after taking care of it so long?

The next day Jared came over, and she met him with a frosty glare.

"What's the matter, Courtney?" Concern etched his face.

She crossed her arms. "I want you to be honest with me."

"I always am. But what do you want to know?"

"Have you been telling people you're selling my house for me?"

"No! Of course not! Why would you believe I would?"

She shook her head. "There's just so many people asking me about it. Did Merrilee tell *that* many people?"

"She probably told a lot of people who told others. Please believe me. I have not told anyone I'm selling your house. If anything, I've told people you're not interested in selling it at this time."

"You promise?"

"Scout's honor."

She relaxed. She wanted to believe him. She had to believe him.

"All right. I believe you."

He swiped his brow. "Whew! If looks could kill, I would've been dead when you opened the door."

"Sorry. I had to be sure."

He took her hand and peered into her eyes. "Courtney, we're friends. Very good friends, I hope. I don't lie to my friends."

The touch of his warm hand and the look in his eyes unnerved her. Yes, he was a very good friend.

"Before I forget it, I need to tell you I'm going away on a two-week TDY starting next week."

"TDY?"

"Air Force jargon for temporary duty assignment."

"Where will you be going?"

"Cannon Air Force Base, New Mexico."

"New Mexico?" A strange hollowness filled her stomach. "That far away?"

"Yep. We practice some things over the desert we can't do around here."

"You sound like you want to go."

His grin spread. "I do. I enjoy flying and look forward to doing it again."

Her gaze swept the room and hopefully hid her reaction to his news. "I hope we'll be finished with our painting before you leave."

"Oh yeah, we will." He stepped to the back door to look at the steps. "These are looking good."

"They definitely do, and they're safer too." She forced her mind on business. "And meet code."

Jared laughed. "Are you going to paint the steps the same color as the porch?"

"Yes, I think white is the best choice. Although that sounds boring with a white house."

"So paint the house a different color, something beachy."

"I could, couldn't I?" She laughed, the tension she'd felt earlier evaporating. "Grandpa would roll over in his grave."

"Maybe not. Just don't go pink."

"Peach?"

"Hmm. Let me think about it. Peach with white trim? That could work."

"Or I could go with a dark blue/gray."

"I like that too. You don't have to make a decision today, do you?"

"No. I'll let it "ruminate," as Grandpa used to say."

As expected, they finished painting the great room and foyer area over the weekend. On Saturday night they celebrated by going to a local seafood place called "Mahi" and listened to the guest musician, a former resident of the area. "I believe he graduated three years before I did," Jared said. "I heard he might buy a house in the area."

"Like birds coming back to roost, aren't we all?"

"Seems like it," Jared said.

When he took her home that night, he said, "So now that the painting is finished, I guess you won't miss me."

Courtney shrugged. "Maybe I will. A little."

He leaned over and kissed her on the forehead, the spot burning from the touch of his lips.

"If something happens and I don't come back, don't forget me."

Fear gripped her. "Is that a possibility?"

"That something will happen, and I don't come back or that you will forget me?"

She punched him lightly in his chest. "You know what I mean."

Jared laughed. "I'm just kidding. Nothing's going to happen."

He kissed her on her cheek, his lips dangerously close to hers. She lifted her face to meet his lips and he pulled her close, kissing her tenderly, then deeply. She reciprocated, drawing him in. When the kiss ended, he drew back. "Wow," he said.

Breathless, she couldn't speak, so he held her close to his chest.

"I'm definitely coming back."

She recovered her voice. "You better."

Chapter Thirteen

Not seeing Jared for the next week created a new kind of loneliness, an emptiness Courtney hadn't expected. After all, she'd been single a long time and was used to doing things by and for herself.

Hank finished his work, so he and his brother were gone too. She loved her new porch, complete with railings all the way around. They had refinished the floor as well, so the place smelled of fresh-cut wood and paint. As she studied her new, open porch, the old furniture looked out of place. Maybe she needed to update that too. Jared was right about how one thing led to another. But should she change the furniture too?

She sat at the picnic table with her iPad and looked for jobs. First she had to update her resume. When she finished that, she decided she might as well go ahead and send some out. None of the jobs or cities where they were located had any real appeal for her, but she had to do something, didn't she? Wasn't it time for her to rejoin the real world?

The effort was more tiring than it should have

been because a nagging voice inside her head kept telling her that she shouldn't be in that situation, that it was Mr. Drake's fault and not hers. She stood and stretched, noticing her neighbor outside.

Mr. Nosy-Pants waved. "Looks a lot better."

"Thanks," she said. "I like it."

"That'll help it sell."

If Courtney could've growled, she would have. Why wouldn't they let that go? She felt like she should put up a "Not for Sale" sign in the front yard.

When her phone rang, she jumped, then her heart did a little flip. Was it Jared?

But the caller was a man who mentioned that his friend, Merrilee, told him he should buy Courtney's house.

"It's not for sale!" She punched disconnect. "That's it. I need to put a stop to this right now!"

Courtney grabbed her purse, and headed to her car, tripping over the sidewalk again. That blasted sidewalk! She had shown it to Hank who said it was probably caused by a root from the magnolia tree.

"You're gonna have to get that root out before it can be fixed," he'd said.

She'd put that on her to-do list for another day.

She climbed into her car and drove to Merrilee's house. She'd never driven there before but knew what community it was in and had no doubt she'd find it, as distinct as it was. Seeing a guardhouse, she hesitated, wondering if he would let her through. But he was on the phone, so she waved at him and smiled, and he opened the gate. She headed to the enormous house and pulled up in the circular driveway, having rehearsed what she would say to the woman on the way.

At the door, Courtney lifted her hand to knock, but a doorbell sounded beyond the door, triggered apparently from her presence. Somewhere in the house, a yippy dog barked. She glanced up to see a camera aimed at her, not surprised the woman had security, living alone in this monstrosity.

She steeled herself to speak at the sound of the lock being moved. As the door slowly opened, Courtney's jaw tensed, ready to let the woman have it, fake friendly smile or not.

But the person in the doorway was not what Courtney expected. Instead of the flamboyant, colorful blonde with ruby lips, Merrilee was dressed in all black, from her tank top to her flowing ruana to her stretch pants. Her hair was a mess, and her lips were colorless. The only color was the black smears down her face and the red eyes. She had been crying.

"What do you want?" she said in a choked-up voice, looking slightly uncomfortable while she held her little growling dog close to her chest. The dog seemed to be the only vestige of strength she possessed at the moment.

Courtney was at a loss for words. She asked herself the same question. What did she want? Vengeance? Against this poor pitiful woman? Her heart sank to her feet.

"I, I, uh, wanted to ask your advice about something." Courtney had no idea where she was going with that comment, but the words had a mind of their own.

Merrilee sniffed and wiped her face. "Advice?"

"Uh, yes." She glanced behind Merrilee. "May I come in a minute?"

"Why don't you ask Jared?" The woman attempted to be surly, but her words didn't have the bite she intended.

"He's out of town. Besides, it's you I need to talk to."

Merrilee quirked an eyebrow and stepped back, sweeping the air with one arm.

Courtney walked in, trying not to gape at the three-story ceiling and amazing chandelier or the glass elevator shaft to one side. The house was impressive, but not garish like she'd expected. In fact, it was tastefully decorated.

"Thank you." Courtney sat on the edge of the closest sofa without being asked.

Merrilee plopped down next to her, setting the dog on the floor that promptly creeped over to Courtney's feet and began sniffing and growling at her shoes. Courtney wanted to ask so badly why the woman was crying, but it wasn't her business.

"You see, I feel like you're trying to get rid of me by telling people I'm selling my house, or that Jared is, when that's not true."

Merrilee stiffened but didn't speak.

"You know, even though I've been here before, right now I'm kind of the new kid in town, and I like it here. I'd like to make friends here too. Is there some reason we can't be friends?"

Merrilee's shoulders slumped, and she began to sob. "I don't have any friends. No one wants to be my friend."

Courtney's heart reached out. "That's not true. I know you have many friends. They've told me so."

Merrilee just shook her head. "No, they're really not friends. They just like me for my money."

"Merrilee, there are many people who want to be your friend if you'll let them. I'm one of them."

Merrilee peered up from under black mascara. "Why? Why do you want to be my friend?"

Courtney prayed for the right answer. "Because we all need friends, people we can count on to be there for us, people who accept us for the way we are, the way God loves us."

More tears ran down Merrilee's face. "I don't know how to be friends. Stan was my only friend, my best friend. All our friends were his friends. After he died, nobody wanted to be my friend anymore."

Courtney didn't know if that was true or not, but the woman was still grieving, and Courtney knew that often people who are grieving push other people away.

"Merrilee, I'm sorry for your loss. It must be very hard to lose someone so close. I've never had a husband, but I remember how hard it was when my grandparents died."

"It's…it's too hard."

"Will you do me a favor?"

"A favor? See what I mean? You want something from me too."

"This kind of favor doesn't cost you anything. Monetarily, at least." Courtney took a deep breath. "Remember I said I needed your advice?"

Merrilee nodded slowly.

"I want you to come to my house and see my new porch. I need to replace the old porch furniture, and I'd like your advice on what to buy." Never in a million years did Courtney think she'd be asking this woman for advice, especially with regards to decorating. *God, did you put those words in my mouth?*

"You really want me to give you decorating advice?"

"Yes, yes I do. Look at how beautifully you've decorated this place." Courtney scanned the room.

"Thank you. Stan told me I had a gift for decorating."

"See? So when can you come? Do you want to come now? You don't need to change or anything. It's just going to be me and you."

Merrilee glanced down at herself. "All right. Just give me a few minutes to freshen up." She stood and beckoned the dog. "Sweet Pea, come with mama." She took a few steps, then turned. "Would you like a drink? I have a bar over there. Help yourself."

"No, thank you. I never drink during the day." If at all. "May I look around while I wait?"

"Sure."

As Merrilee left the room, Courtney stood and stared out the huge glass windows that looked onto the beach. What just happened? She had invited someone to her house. For advice. Someone she didn't even like. She chuckled. *God, you have a sense of humor, don't you?*

When Merrilee came back a few minutes later, she had cleaned her face and brushed her hair.

She'd also put on her red lipstick and a gold necklace and earrings.

"Shall we go in my car? I'll bring you back when we're finished."

"All right. May I bring Sweet Pea? I hate to leave her alone."

"Sure, I don't think Tucker will mind." Thank God, Tucker was a nice dog.

At Courtney's, Merrilee scanned the yard and the house. No doubt she was sizing up the problems with the house. "Watch your step," Courtney said, as they navigated the walkway. "I'm going to get that fixed soon."

She remembered Hanks words about the sidewalk. "You've got to cut that root out before you can fix it." A Bible verse tugged at the edges of Courtney's mind as she led Merrilee into the house.

Inside, Merrilee's eyes roamed the interior. "I just painted the walls." Courtney left out the part about Jared helping.

"Nice color," Merrilee said.

Courtney led her through the house and out to the porch. "So you see what I have. Can you recommend something more refreshing?"

Merrilee stood on the porch, Sweet Pea in her arms, and surveyed the area. Tucker sat nearby, as he and the little dog stayed focused on each other. Courtney wondered what would happen if the dog was put down on the floor. No, better not.

"Let me think about it. Do you have a color scheme in mind?"

"Other than the blue in the living room, not really. Although I have thought about repainting the whole exterior of the house. I just don't know what color yet."

"All right. I'll do some searching and let you know what I come up with."

"That would be great!" Courtney motioned back toward the kitchen. "Can I get you anything? Coffee? Water? Tea?"

Merrilee frowned and shook her head. Then she said, "You have tea?"

"Yes. I made it myself. It's not as sweet as my mother makes it, but it's sweet. Is that all right?"

Merrilee offered a little smile. "I've always loved sweet tea, but it's been a long time since I've had any, must less made it."

Courtney poured them each a glass of tea, then they went back to the porch and sat at the picnic table. As they let the sea breeze and the sound of the gentle surf soften the air around them, Merrilee relaxed and began talking about her past. Courtney learned that the woman had grown up very poor in the country and hadn't had much education but had always loved colors and had a flair for design. She'd been working in a grocery store when she met Stan. She'd flirted with the widower and soon they were married. Stan had fulfilled all her dreams and given her everything she'd ever wanted except for children. But the two of them were very happy before he had a heart attack and died.

As she talked, Courtney saw a different woman, not the one that pretended to be someone else, the original, simple woman. All her pretenses had disappeared, and only her southern accent remained the same. Courtney liked this new woman, and as they talked, an idea formed in her mind.

After she took Merrilee home, Courtney took a pad of paper and walked around the house, sketching and taking notes. Upstairs and downstairs, she walked as a vision came together. And as the vision clarified, her excitement built. She knew what she wanted to do.

Chapter Fourteen

Jared sat in his car, watching the sun set and stealing the first opportunity he'd had since arriving in New Mexico to call Courtney. He hadn't wanted to waste another minute driving to the VOQ— Visiting Officer Quarters, aka the base hotel— before calling. And he was glad he hadn't waited, because she was bubbling with excitement.

"Sorry I haven't called before. By the time we're finished, it's late, and I know we're two hours behind you, so I didn't want to call so late."

"It's okay. I've been busy."

"Yeah? Doing what? More painting? Without me?" He kept his tone light, though he felt a twinge of sadness at the idea. Of course, the woman could do something on her own.

"Not yet." She sounded like she was holding something back.

"What's going on, Courtney?" His pulse increased. Was she getting ready to leave?

She giggled. "Merrilee came over today?"

"What? No way. Did she insult you?"

"No, actually, I invited her."

"Okay, Courtney. I give. What's going on?"

Courtney explained to him about how she went to Merrilee's house to tell her off, then how she changed her mind and she felt God led her to reach out to Merrilee as a friend. She told him about asking for Merrilee's advice and how the woman had opened up to her.

"She's really a nice person, once you get to know the real Merrilee."

"Amazing. You sound happy." He smiled, her mood infectious, even over the phone.

"I am, like a weight's been lifted from my shoulders."

"That's good to hear. I've been praying that you could let go of the negative people in your life."

"You mean, like my former boss too?"

"Well, I wasn't going to say it, but yes, him too."

"I'm over him. God showed me something."

"What?"

"I'll tell you when you get back."

"I can't wait."

"For me to tell you?"

"No, to get back to you. I really miss you." Since he'd been gone, thoughts of her had seldom been far from his mind, and he suspected his feelings were deeper than friendship.

"I miss you too."

"Not as much as I miss you." He baited her.

She laughed. "How do you know?"

"Guess we'll find out when I get back."

"Guess we will."

After the call, Jared's mind went back to the kiss they'd shared before he left. He touched his lips, wishing hers were touching them instead. Just a few more days and they would be, if he had anything to do with it.

~

When Jared pulled up in front of Courtney's house, he found Hank out front working on the walkway.

"Hey Hank! Glad to see that's getting fixed."

"Me too. Somebody was gonna fall and hurt themselves."

Courtney stepped outside and when their gazes met, she sprang down the steps and into Jared's arms.

"I've missed you so much!" She laced her hands behind his neck.

He searched her eyes, then lowered his mouth to hers and drew her into a kiss, hoping he conveyed as much feeling as he could in a kiss.

Then he lifted his head and exhaled. "Man. I've missed you." Realizing they were standing near Hank with this public show of affection, he nodded to the sidewalk. "I see you're getting that sidewalk fixed."

Courtney grinned and linked her arm into his, pulling him toward the front door.

"That's what God showed me."

He glanced back at the sidewalk. "God wanted you to fix the sidewalk?"

She laughed and nodded. "You see, Hank told me the sidewalk couldn't be fixed before the tree root that was under it was cut away. Unless the root was removed, the sidewalk would never be level."

"Yes, that's true."

"God reminded me of a Bible verse. 'See to it that no one falls short of the grace of God and that no bitter root grows up to cause trouble and defile many.' You see, I had the root of bitterness in my heart. I was bitter about my job loss, about Merrilee, about being told what to do. I had to get rid of that bitterness before it caused more trouble in my life. I needed to show grace and forgiveness instead. So I let God cut that bitter root out of me."

Jared hugged her. "I'm so happy to hear that, Courtney."

She led him into the house and out to the porch where he viewed the changes.

"New furniture too?"

"Yes, isn't it pretty? Merrilee picked it out for me."

The bright floral pattern in peach, aqua and blue brightened the porch and coordinated with the color of the water.

He put his arm around her. "You're just full of surprises today."

"That's not all." Her grin was impish.

"There's more? What else/"

She led him to the kitchen table where a series of sketches were laid out. She picked up one, a picture of a sign.

"You are now standing in the Serenity Bed and Breakfast!"

His eyes rounded and his mouth dropped open. "You're turning this house into a B & B?"

She nodded, her eyes twinkling as her smile stretched across her face. "Yes, sir. I've got the zoning changed and the approval to move ahead.

Construction begins next week."

"Courtney, that's fabulous!" He hugged her again, lifting her off her feet.

As he set her back down on the floor, he leaned in to kiss her again.

"So that means you're not going away again?"

She shook her head. "Nope. I'm planning to be here a long time."

"That's the best news I've heard yet."

His lips took hers and he kissed her as if she was the most important person in his life. Actually, she was.

Award-winning author Marilyn Turk writes historical fiction flavored with suspense and romance. Marilyn also writes devotions for Daily Guideposts. She and her husband are lighthouse enthusiasts, have visited over 100 lighthouses and also served as volunteer lighthouse caretakers at Little River Light off the coast of Maine.

When not writing or visiting lighthouses, Marilyn enjoys walking, boating, fishing, gardening, tennis, playing with grandkids and her golden retriever Dolly.

She is a member of American Christian Fiction Writers, Faith, Hope and Love, Advanced Writers and Speakers Association, Word Weavers International, and the United States Lighthouse Society.

Facebook –
https://www.facebook.com/marilyn.turk.9/
Twitter – @marilynturk.com
Pinterest -
https://www.pinterest.com/bluewaterbayou.
Website – Pathways of the Heart,
https://pathwayheart.com/. Two blogs: Lighthouse blog and The Writers Path blog. Sign up for newsletter and blogs on this site.
Bookbub -
https://www.bookbub.com/profile/marilyn-turk
Goodreads -
https://www.goodreads.com/author/show/9791210.

Marilyn_Turk

Amazon author page -

https://www.amazon.com/Marilyn-Turk/e/B017Y76L9A

Books by Marilyn Turk

Historical Series

Coastal Lights Legacy
Rebel Light
Revealing Light
Redeeming Light
Rekindled Light

Suspicious Shores
The Gilded Curse
Shadowed by a Spy
Seaside Strangers (coming soon)

Standalone Novels
Abigail's Secret

Novella Collections
The Wrong Survivor in *Great Lakes Lighthouse Brides*
Love's Cookin' at the Cowboy Café in *Crinoline Cowboys*
Between Two Worlds in *Heart of the Midwife*
The Christmas Gift in *The Christmas Gazebo*
Kaetlyn's Cup of Christmas Cheer in *Misstletoe Mishaps*
Not My Party in *Never Too Late for Romance*
Book Lady of the Bayou in *The Librarian's Journey*
(coming soon)

Nonfiction
Lighthouse Devotions

Would you like to read more of Marilyn's books?

Misstletoe Mishaps
A collection of humorous historical holiday novellas.
<u>Y</u>
Kaetlyn's Cup of Christmas Cheer, part of *Misstletoe Mishaps*
https://www.amazon.com/Kaetlyns-Cup-Christmas-Cheer-Novella-ebook/dp/B08KJD9S9J

The Christmas Gazebo
Romance is in the air when two couples - 100 years apart - encounter the spirit of Christmas at the same Victorian mansion.

Rebel Light, Coastal Lights Legacy, Book 1
Civil War has begun in Florida and Kate MacFarland runs away from the war only to find herself in the middle of it. Who will protect her now?

Revealing Light, Coastal Lights Legacy, Book 2
Sally Rose McFarlane follows her dream of being a teacher when she accepts a position as governess in post-Reconstruction, Florida. A misunderstanding of her previous experience in Ohio and the new Jim Crow laws forces her to keep her bi-racial heritage a secret in order to keep her job.

Redeeming Light, Coastal Lights Legacy, Book 3

Cora Miller's millinery business is doing well in 1875 St. Augustine until jewelry from her wealthy customers begins to disappear and then mysteriously reappear in Cora's shop.

Rekindled Light, Coastal Lights Legacy, Book 4

At the onset of the Civil War, Sarah Turner's hope to marry fiancé Josiah Hamilton crumbled when her father forbade her to ever see Josiah again because he chose the Union side. Now the war has ended, and Sarah and her family return to Pensacola to start life over. Little does she know that Josiah is there as well to rebuild the Pensacola lighthouse. Can their love be rekindled despite the years and separation they've endured, especially when an arsonist is determined to keep them apart?

Coastal Lights Legacy, collection of all four novels.

Marilyn would love to connect with you at any of the below social media sites.

Facebook: https://www.facebook.com/marilyn.turk.9

Twitter: https://twitter.com/MarilynTurk

Pinterest: https://pinterest.com/bluewaterbayou/

Email: marilynturkwriter@yahoo.com

Amazon Author Page: https://www.amazon.com/Marilyn-Turk/e/B017Y76L9A/

Sign up for Forget Me Not Romances newsletter and receive a special gift compiled from Forget Me Not Authors!

Join our FB pages to keep up on our most current news!